Bourbon & BLISS

USA TODAY BESTSELLING AUTHOR
ZEE IRWIN

xoxo

Zee ♡

BOURBON & BLISS

A STEAMY SMALL TOWN ROCK STAR
ROMANCE

WELCOME TO KISSING SPRINGS: THE
BOURBON SEASON

ZEE IRWIN

CER CREATIVE COMPANY PUBLISHING, LLC

Cover Model from: Wander Photography

Editing/proofing: JAL Editing

To autumn walks in a small town, hand-in-hand with someone you love.

Get a Free Story

xoxo

Hello!

My books are feel good steamy romance. If you love billionaire romance, steamy small town romance, military or cowboy romance, then you've come to the right author! :)

Stay in touch. I'll have a FREE story for you:

ZeeIrwinAuthor.com/series

Content Warnings

Dear Readers:

I don't often feel the need to include warnings in my stories, but this particular set of characters grapple with some real-life issues. While I touch on these things lightly, I hope I told their stories with all the grace and dignity they deserved. You'll read about:

Emotional abuse from a parent

Stalking

Held captive by someone

A crime scene involving a cold case murder

Missing family members

Death of a loved one due to cancer

Thank you for reading.

CHAPTER 1

JUST A FIERCE GIRL

PRIMA SIMMS, THE ROCK STAR DIVA

"A DIVORCE CONCERT? REALLY?" Sara frowned and complained. "I don't like the sound of this one bit."

I stuck my nose in the air and tried to remain true to my idea of celebrating my divorce with an exclusive concert right here in Kissing Springs. My twin sister was the one person in this world who knew me the best. So why couldn't she understand my need to wash a certain man out of my hair?

"Bruce MacMillan proved to be the worst mistake of my life —why can't you see that?" I came back at her.

Sara was the one who introduced us, but I wouldn't hold it against her, of course. Neither of us could have predicted the lengths Bruce would go to during my marriage trying to control my career, my money, my life.

"I spent the entire summer down and bitter about the divorce, not to mention having to deal with what Mom did to me." I was still coming to terms with how the two people I trusted most—my ex-husband and my mother—used me and hurt me. A shudder worked through me thinking about it all, but I refused to show any weakness.

"Now I'm late getting a new album done, and I gained ten pounds from all the stress and worry. I'm nearly broke, fighting to keep my career alive, while battling all the social media naysayers that I'm a washed up has-been," I retorted.

I glanced around the boardroom at the Derby Nights Entertainment Group headquarters. Sara held hands with her new fiancé Charles Montgomery on one side of the table, while his brother Dillon sat on the other side next to his soon-to-be bride, Mayor Meadow Boyd. While Sara and Charles hadn't set a date yet, Meadow and Dillon set their nuptials for Thanksgiving weekend.

Everyone had someone. Except me and Robbie Boyd, the hot chief of police. He sat opposite me at the other end. What a fine specimen of a man, the epitome of tall, dark-haired, blue-eyed, and handsome. His perfect build and looks could easily make me forget my ex.

Bruce neglected me for so long. Now that I have a taste of freedom again, it's time for some fun. I'd been a rock star diva all of my life, and none of these people in the room would deter me from getting what I wanted.

"Excuse me if I want to have a celebration of freedom, now that the divorce is final, and put this entire chapter of my life behind me. A concert to party with my fans is the best idea

I've ever had." I crossed my arms as if that was my final say on the matter.

"Prima, I'm just concerned. You've been through so much this summer, plus these threats you've received by email through your fan club are getting more and more scary. I asked Robbie here today to look into them." Sara pleaded with her eyes. "All things considered, I don't think right now is the time for a public display like a concert."

I stood my ground. "Are you kidding? It's the *best* time." I grabbed my phone and swiped through photos. "Look, I even have the perfect dress. Red, off the shoulder, cinched at the waist with a corset, ruffled hem, and split up the leg— Add a pair of red leather cowboy boots and I'll look stunning and fierce."

With my phone in hand, I walked around the table and showed everyone. When I got to Robbie, he hardly noticed, but peered up into my eyes instead.

What I saw in them made my breath hitch. Deep in his *gorgeous* blues resided a man who possibly understood me.

"I commend your spirit." he nodded. "Breakups are never easy, and everyone has to find their own ways of dealing with it. Hell, Meadow once burned all of Josh's flannel shirts in her yard after their break up—"

"Robbie, shush." Meadow chastised her brother. "Prima, while I agree with him about doing what you need to for healing, I'm not sure a concert celebrating divorce is the best image for Kissing Springs as the Romance Capital of the South."

"Actually, I like where this is headed." All eyes turned to Charles, who shocked me with his support.

While Charles had been an amazing help in sending me money when Bruce cleared out our joint accounts prior to our divorce, I was still getting used to the idea that he'd soon be my brother-in-law.

He leaned forward, as if taking a keen interest. "It's a wild idea, something different, yes. But I'm kind of getting a vision. I don't know why, but I see you in that red dress by the springs burning a wedding photo. Might make an awesome rock 'n roll album cover."

Mick Magnus, the owner of Wild Horses Music, cleared his throat, his voice breaking in from the conference call device in the center of the table. "I feel it too. You *are* branded *Prima The Rock Star Diva,* after all. Music fans have come to expect the unexpected from you over the years, and nothing says over the top like a divorce celebration." I loved Mick. As the head of Wild Horses Music, now partnering with Dillon's Derby Nights group, I hoped he'd be on my side.

Mutt Blainey, long-time friend and producer of several of my past hits, chimed in over the conference call as well, his voice rushed in excitement. "Shit, this is the inspiration we needed. Prima, you know that tune you were in the middle of writing about being down and out losing your man? How about this? We start out slow, sounding like it's going to be a *woe is me* type of tune. We pause, then bash them over the head with wild rock riffs and lyrics with a crazy attitude. Like *Hell yeah, he's gone,* type of thing."

His support was more than encouraging. I took in a deep breath and closed my eyes, trying to picture it all.

Suddenly, words and tunes hit me, flowing in bits and pieces. All my unfinished depressing songs from the summer reformed with an edgier rock 'n roll vibe. Hell, yes.

When I opened my eyes, I didn't need a mirror to know the twinkle was back. A smile split my face. "Yes! Finally, my muse has returned with a solid direction to get this album finished."

Relief spread around the room from face to face, like an energy that palpitated with new life. Renewed in spirit, I was eager to immerse myself back into my work, even if it had to be here in this Podunk small town at the new Wild Horses Music Studios.

"Hell yeah. Let's rock and roll," Mutt exclaimed. "I'll take the next flight out and be there by morning. We need to get into the studio and work with this muse while we can."

"I'll get the marketing team on this and book the best photographer right away," Mick added.

Sara came to me with a hug. "I love the new direction for the album, Prim. I'm so excited for you."

Even Meadow sounded pleased as well. "Wonderful idea to turn the divorce concert idea into the album cover instead. Whew, looks like Kissing Springs will still be all about celebrating love."

I parted from Sara. "Oh no, I'm still having a damn concert. I *will* celebrate love—for myself. Book the Boyd Theater for me, Dillon. I'm going to rock that place in my red dress if it's the last thing I do."

I ignored the look on Meadow's face, certain that a concert would bring in more exposure to the town she loved so dearly.

"Sorry to burst your bubble," Robbie stood and approached me.

"Feel free to burst in anytime." I batted my eyes, rewarded by a curve of his lips on one side.

"The concert sounds wild, but there's a part of me that hopes you'll proceed with caution. I'm a cop, after all and safety should be the biggest concern," he said. "These threats you've been getting need looking into, but they shouldn't keep you from doing what you want. We'll just have to beef up security around you."

"Oh, I assure you. I always get what I want." I stepped closer, eyeing his tall—beefy—build. "I hope I can count on you to protect me, sheriff?"

"Uh, it's just chief, not sheriff." He winked. "When do you plan on having this?" He asked, shifting close to me as well. His heady aftershave surrounded me like a glove.

"Halloween night."

"What?" Dillon's reaction across the room surprised me. "This is the middle of September, Prima. You're not giving us a lot of time."

"Mick, tell me you'll make this happen. Surely everything can be fast-tracked?" I shouted at the conference call device in the center of the table with my hands on my hips.

He'd better say yes. I want this damn concert more than anything.

"Now Prima, listen. Why don't you let Dillon and I discuss this? We'll talk with our teams and get back to you by the morning, okay?"

"Talk all you like, but I *will* have my concert when I want it."

Sara pulled me aside by my arm. "Prim, play nice. You can't just expect these people to fall in line with your demands."

"Why not? I saw how fast they put together the street fair and music festival this summer. My concert will be much easier considering it'll be at the Boyd Theater and not out in the streets with fifty vendors," I defended myself.

"But it's all happening so fast. I worry about you. After Mom held you captive and your divorce and everything. I think you'd be better taking some time off."

My insides cringed at her concerns. The thought of our mother, Lucy, and what she did to me over the summer, luring me back into her clutches, holding me against my will, thinking she could take over managing my career—I'd yet to have a restful night's sleep.

As for Bruce, I was long over my ex-husband before the ink on our divorce dried, and all that remained was anger and resentment. And a stalker? Psh. I'd had plenty of those over the years and I was still standing here.

These things might be enough to keep any sane person down and out for a while. But not me. Not now. I refused to let them.

I shook it off, tossing my hair. "Nonsense. I'm fine. Screw Lucy, Bruce, and the stalker. No one will ever again hold me back."

Enough was enough.

I prepared for the world's greatest come back on stage, mustering the old me, the one who was just a fierce girl fighting for everything she wanted.

This time, no one and nothing would stand in my way.

CHAPTER 2

LOST A PIECE OF MY HEART

ROBBIE BOYD, CHIEF OF POLICE

I HAD ONE RULE: Never get personally attached to a case.

The one time I did, I lost a piece of my heart. It took everything in me not to think about that.

I wasn't some asshole cop. Of course I cared about the people in my community. But the line I tried not to cross got thinner every day. Today, it vanished.

"Good afternoon. Thanks for joining us today for this press conference," I began, and addressed a room dotted with reporters, family, and friends. "After the fire that burned down the old Brown Jug Bar, excavators uncovered the remains of a body. Thanks to DNA testing, we discovered it was Fannie Boyd. Fannie disappeared at age eighteen, and has been a cold case ever since."

My father's sister went out to meet her boyfriend one night, and neither was ever seen or heard from again. The mystery, now decades old, was one of my family's great tragedies, even greater than the old Boyd and Montgomery family feud of Kissing Springs' lore.

Gasps rose from a few of the dozen news reporters in the room as I held tight to the paper I was reading from like it contained the story of my life. The click of a few camera shutters couldn't drown out the sobs from the front row.

"Oh, Fannie," Aunt Minnie cried. Uncle Jeb, was her rock, handing her a handkerchief and holding her tight. We'd lost my father and mother under tragic circumstances, and now Fannie.

I'd join Jeb in hugging her, too, but remained strong at the podium as the Police Chief, with the Boyd family mystery on display for the entire world to see.

I glanced at Prima seated a few spots from them in the front row, and it still shocked me to see a world-famous rock star here in my small town. Her hair, the color of dark magenta, framed her creamy skin and set off a pair of beguiling green eyes.

A hundred things intrigued me about her, but as much as her beauty captivated me from the minute she stepped foot here, I had a job to do.

Ever since news spread that Prima was staying locally for a while, suddenly Kissing Springs was on the radar of the stations in Louisville, Lexington, and beyond. Just last week, I spotted news trucks from Chicago and St. Louis driving up and down Main Street as if they were scouting for signs of her.

Last year, they wouldn't have cared much about Kissing Springs. The story of a body found under a burned down bar, would have simply made our local newspaper maybe a mention in the city papers. Today, I'm standing at a podium with half a dozen microphones in my face.

I cleared my throat and swallowed my pride as I read the next sentence. "I want to thank Charles Montgomery, owner of the Brown Jug Bar, for his cooperation in this effort to retrieve the body."

I motioned to my right, where he and his brother Dillon stood. They'd better not think I was done with them; plenty of questions swirled around their family involvement in this.

"And thanks goes to the Louisville special task force. With their help, when excavators uncovered the remains after the bar fire, we were able to work quickly to retrieve all the evidence. The speed at which they worked and processed DNA got us to this point, and we're grateful. And now, Mayor Meadow Boyd would like to say a few words."

As I stepped back from the podium to give my pregnant sister space, she hugged me. "Thank you, Chief Boyd. This is indeed a sad day for our family."

Her hand remained on her growing baby bump as she spoke. "When I took over as mayor, I promised a new day for the residents of Kissing Springs. While we mourn about the past, we must remain strong and look ahead to our future and not lose sight of all that we've built this year."

As she outlined the events happening in town this fall, all the credit went to her for doing what she'd set out to do. As my patrol officers had been reporting to me, they'd observed a renewed spirit among the townsfolk here.

My sister was one hard-working mayor, but with her wedding to Dillon coming up and her baby soon after that, it was hard to say how much longer she could keep up.

"As a community, we will grieve and heal and move past this. Please join me in helping to keep Kissing Springs strong for a better future. And now, back to Chief Boyd," Meadow concluded.

I stepped up. "We only have time for a few questions." Ten hands flew into the air. I sighed and pointed to the nearest one, a tall man from one of the Lexington stations.

"Do you have any theories yet on what might have happened to Fannie Boyd?" he asked.

"Not yet. This is a cold case file that's been frozen far too long. My department has to start from square one, open it back up, review the work done on it over the years. It'll be a process." Hands went up again, and I pointed to the left at Amelia from our local newspaper.

"Given the long-standing feud between the Boyds and Montgomery's, how much does it factor into the investigation?"

I side eyed Dillon and Charles. "Well, as you know, Amelia, Mayor Boyd and Dillon Montgomery are about to be married, joining our two families together. I'd like to think this generation has come a long way toward healing the sins of the past. As I said, the Montgomerys are cooperating with the investigation."

The brothers better fucking continue cooperating or I'd give them hell.

Dillon was okay, and I'd come to accept his love for my sister as true. But Charles? I was still on the fence about him, even though last week he'd announced a huge donation and plans to improve the Kissing Springs Park, turning it into a nicer attraction for local families.

He's great at making a public show of his good deeds. It's what he did behind closed doors that worried me. Although, to his credit, he'd managed to run the worst of his Montgomery cousins out of town this summer.

I didn't know the details of how he made that happen, and probably better that way.

The Montgomerys had always been trouble from the moment they stepped foot on this land, stealing the claim from the Boyd's in the 1800s. But, for Meadow's sake, I tried to put the feud behind me. Like she was famous for saying, that was our past, but didn't have to be our future.

I pointed to a man at the back. "Final question."

"According to my research, Mac Granger was the chief of police around the time of Fannie's disappearance. Will he be brought in and involved in the new investigation?"

My jaw clicked. "I think we can find everything we need in our archives. Mac was known for keeping meticulous records. I don't see a need to disturb his retirement. That's it for now. Please direct any other questions to my department. Thanks."

While we all made our way out of the room and into the anteroom, I hesitated upon hearing some reporters shouting questions to Prima. I turned at the door to yell at them to leave her alone, but she managed like a pro, smiling, tossing her hair behind her shoulder, and obviously comfortable with the attention.

"How is your new album coming along?" One asked, holding his recorder very close to her mouth.

"Swimmingly," she said. "Everyone at Wild Horses Music has been incredible to work with. I'm truly honored to be here in Kissing Springs."

"Do you have a date set yet for when it will be released?" Another asked.

"Soon. We're hard at work and I can't wait to put it out. Maybe before Christmas? But I will have some exciting news about a special concert, so stay tuned."

As she took a few more questions, the beauty handled herself well, and I stood there, mesmerized. Her long legs, accentuated by black stiletto boots that ended mid-thigh, could make a grown man happy if they were wrapped around his waist.

With an ass like a peach in tight faded jeans, I was grateful her backside was facing me until she turned enough to see me standing there ogling her.

The corner of her mouth lifted, and I couldn't deny the chemistry between us. But I should stop right there and keep myself in check. As big a fan as I was of her music, and although being around her fulfilled some sort of fantasy about being with a rock star, she was only in town for a short time.

My life was here. Hers was in a universe of stardom I couldn't even begin to fathom and understand.

CHAPTER 3

WHAT WOULD LOVE HAVE TO DO WITH IT?

ROBBIE

AFTER THE PRESS CONFERENCE, I retreated into the anteroom and closed the door behind me, overhearing Dillon speaking low to Charles.

"Maybe you should have made all this go away like Uncle Ogden warned," he said.

I rushed them. "What the fuck are you two talking about?" Neither spoke up, so I pointed a finger at them. "Don't think for a minute I'm not watching your every move. If you even think to fuck with this investigation—"

"Well, I could have easily caused a landslide out at the bar site, making it unsafe and a hundred times harder to pull out the body and evidence." Charles seethed, then smiled. "But I didn't, did I?"

"Robbie, please, this is not the time for another family feud to start," Meadow begged, holding onto Aunt Minnie, who broke down into tears again.

"Listen to your sister, chief." Charles could be such an asshole, always had been since high school. "Like it or not, I'm a permanent resident of Kissing Springs now. My twins go to school here, Sara and I will wed here at Christmas, and with a new set of twins on the way, we're here to stay. Oh, and I almost forgot, once Dillon and Meadow marry, I get to call you family."

I looked around at all of them and yanked at the tie of my uniform to loosen it. What a lot we were, the Boyds and Montgomerys. Our ancestors must be rolling in their graves, laughing like hell, seeing us all in one room together.

"Fine," I grumbled. "Just stay out of my way, Charles. Don't impede my investigation, unless you have anything to add to it, like a sworn confession from one of your relatives who did this to Fannie."

"You automatically assume it was our side who did this?" Dillon stepped forward, turning red.

Charles scoffed. "The fact is, this case couldn't be solved under Mac's authority, and I hear he was an excellent investigator at one time before he turned into an alcoholic and was forced to retire. The case probably won't be solved under yours, either."

His smug mug as he spoke made me sick. I should punch him in the face for talking about Mac like that. He never knew the old chief like I did, and I'd be damned to stand here and listen to another minute of this.

"But don't worry. As a law-abiding, upstanding citizen of Kissing Springs, if I hear of anything that will help, you'll be the first to know. Now, if you'll excuse me, I'm off to enjoy this beautiful fall day with my fiancée and my daughters at the new park ground breaking ceremony." As Charles left with a grin on his face, I wished for rain to pour on his head.

"Can you get Minnie home?" Meadow passed our aunt into Jeb's arms. "I have to appear at the park ceremony, but then I'll fill in at the pie shop for her until closing."

"I'll come, too, sweetheart," Dillon offered, and they all shuffled out the door, leaving me behind, which was fine by me. Glad for a little peace and quiet to help me think, I ran my hands through my hair. None of this sat right in my gut.

I strode through the small station back to my office and psyched myself up for the grueling task of opening the old evidence in Aunt Fannie's case. My steps faltered though, seeing Prima through the glass, waiting for me.

Fuck, I wished my guys wouldn't have let her in. She's a damn sexy distraction at a terrible time right now.

I entered and shut the door behind me. "Hi, Prima. Thanks for attending the press conference."

"Sure. I'm sorry to hear the news about your family today."

"Yeah, thanks. What can I help you with?" I sat behind my desk, mainly to hide something growing in my pants, as she sat opposite me with her cleavage on full display. In a flirty white off-shoulder blouse, that much creamy skin exposed should be a crime. I could cuff her and take her in a heartbeat.

As she leaned forward, her breasts swelled, and her nipples pebbled through the fabric. Biting her bottom lip wasn't helping deter the fan-crush I'd always had on the rock star. I needed to separate the fantasy from the reality, and fast, to keep things professional.

"I wondered if you gave more thought to my security plan? I'm relying on you to keep me out of harm's way during my upcoming concert." Her voice purred, soft like velvet, as opposed to the rasp of her rock and roll sound. This woman was such a contradiction between her wild stage persona and the sexy kitten she could be offstage.

The younger man inside of me went crazy with the rock star fantasies, but the mature guy who'd been around a block or two, failing at love, rather enjoyed her tame—hopefully real —personality. Both appealed to me equally.

I shifted in my seat and cleared my throat. This was no way for the Chief of Police to be acting.

"I'm waiting for a few more details from Mick and Dillon. As soon as I have those, I'll draft up a plan. Don't worry, my people will keep you safe."

"People? I thought *you'd* be the one...watching over me." Her lashes fluttered and the jewels in her eyes drew me in deeper than I should dive.

"Oh, I'll be keeping an eye on you. You're hard to miss." I dared flirt back, and considering her divorce was very recent, that's as far as this should go. More than one red flag surrounded this woman.

In all the self-help books I'd read since my last breakup, Prima was, without a doubt, the one they warned me about. Untamed, needy, and ripe from heartbreak...yeah, she was the poster image for *Woman on the Rebound*.

She stood and handed me a card. "Here's my number then. When you get the plans together, call me. We'll have dinner and...talk." With an intoxicating smile filled with nuance, she sashayed out of the room.

Only when my eyes could no longer watch her peach-ass once she turned the corner to exit the building did I glance down at the card. It simply said *Prima* with her phone number, and a row of Xs and Os beneath it. The dot above the *i* was in the shape of a heart.

Something told me while protecting her, I'd need to put a suit of armor around the organ that's beating wildly in my chest—and one around my cock wouldn't hurt, too.

For her, while the ink was barely dry on her divorce papers, her fiercely independent exterior couldn't hide the one thing from me I knew was lurking beneath the surface...pain. I'd be nothing but a shoulder for her to cry on, and a quick fuck before she moved on and left this small town.

I mean, that'd be fun as hell, but...

For me, it'd been a couple of long years since my ex broke up with me. I had issues, according to her, and she was right. The only way I could see to deal with them was through a forced break from the dating scene—what little we had here in Kissing Springs.

I guess I had reached a point where I just didn't want to bother with a relationship, no matter how much the old biddies in town raised the bet to see if I'd ever get hitched.

Instead, I developed an unhealthy obsession with self-help books. Through a lot of reading, a lot of thinking, and a whole hell of a lot of Kentucky bourbon, eventually, I set my head straight on who I was and what I wanted in a woman.

Now? I was open and ready to date and find love again. Watching my sister settle down with Dillon had put a lot of thoughts into my head. When I found the right woman, our home, our careers, our lives would be here.

I didn't quite see how a rock star would fit into that picture. No, anything with Prima would be only about sex; what would love have to do with a rock star passing through town?

I reached for the box of Fannie's cold case files and set it square in the center of my desk. It was time to put all thoughts of Prima out of my head and focus on my duty to my family and my town.

CHAPTER 4
SO WHAT IF I'M A ROCK STAR
PRIMA

"OH, YEAH!" I finished the rocking tune with a screech at the top of my vocal range, then I peeked at Mutt in the control room. We'd been at it all afternoon, putting the finishing touches on one of my revamped songs.

"Nice one. I'd like to see you hold that last note for a few beats, though." His direction came through the speakers.

"Thanks. Yeah, I agree. In fact, let's roll back to that last chorus for another take. I heard a tremble in my voice. I know I can do better."

"Wow. Who are you, and what have you done with Prima?" His gray eyebrows arched.

"What do you mean?" I laughed him off.

"Your recording sessions in the past typically lasted a few hours, and, well, you rarely agreed with me. Here in Kissing Springs, all week long, you've been congenial, and putting in eight to twelve solid hours."

I reached for my herbal tea with ginger, lemon, and honey, the perfect remedy to keep my vocals hydrated. "I'm a rock star, so I'm revved up to get this new material ready for the concert."

"Hm. No. I notice something different in you. There's a soul to your sound that wasn't there before." His observation wasn't wrong.

"Well, I've been through a lot over the past year. Guess I've grown up." A few swallows of the tea coated my cords really well. "And look at us, not at each other's throats. This is definitely progress. Remember that one time in L.A. when I had you removed from the studio by security?"

His laughter rolled through the speaker, and only with the benefit of hindsight could I laugh about it now, too. Mutt was one of the best producers in the business, but we'd had our arguments about my work in the past.

The door to the room opened, ending our talk when Mick Magnus walked in. "Hey strangers."

"Mick?" I rushed from the booth and entered the control room on the opposite side. "Hey yourself. I wondered if I'd ever see you in person again." I hugged him, or rather, his torso.

Well over six feet, he towered about a foot taller than me. As the youngest of the Magnus brothers, and with his dimples, he was easy on the eyes.

We'd met at a party a few years back when he was still with his father's Magnus Music conglomerate, and I'd kept my eye on his career ever since.

After Mr. Magnus died, Mick and Jimmy, one of his brothers, stepped out on their own, creating Wild Horses Music. My intuition told me I should work with them, and usually I'm right.

As I pulled away, Robbie stepped into the room, too. "Hi Prima." He nodded, sending me a smoldering smile that wet my panties.

"Hi. Well, lucky me. Three handsome men in one tiny room." I cracked a joke, sort of. I always enjoyed being the center of male attention. "What brings you two here?"

"I wanted to deliver the news personally. Tickets to your exclusive Halloween Alive and Kicking concert sold out in less than an hour," Mick gushed.

"What? Woohoo," I high-fived everyone.

"Prima is back, ladies and gentlemen," Mutt put a hand around my arm, squeezed and released it.

"Yes, it's great news, but we have much work to do now. We have a security meeting today, so I drove up from Nashville to make sure my best artist will be safe at her concert on Halloween night." Mick winked at me. "Robbie, have you met Mutt?"

The two men shook hands, looking like such an odd pairing. Robbie was a tall drink of cool water in his police uniform, compared to Mutt's short stature with long gray hair and wearing a Hawaiian shirt.

"Hi. What an honor to meet the man behind the Loose Leopard's latest album," Robbie said, impressing me with his knowledge of rock and roll.

"Thanks. That's some of my best work. Of course, it took an obscene amount of drugs to get the best out of those jerks," Mutt cackled.

"Uh. That's probably something you shouldn't be telling a police officer." I cocked my head.

"I'm joking, seriously."

"I'll pretend I didn't hear that." Robbie gave him a stern look. "But I've never seen the inside of a studio before. I heard some of the track you were working on in the hallway before we came in, Prima." Robbie thumbed behind him. "It sounds great. Can't wait to hear the completed album."

"Well, since I know you're a fan of my music, I'll be sure to send you an advanced copy of it, just so I can get your *personal* opinion." Was I coming on strong?

I couldn't help it. The man didn't belong in a small town, but in Hollywood as a total hottie, heating up the movie screens. Women would go crazy for him—then again, maybe he's best staying right here, where only I could ogle him.

"Yeah? I'll give it a listen." The way his eyes crinkled at the edges and trained on me had my stomach flipping worse than that time I met one of the Backstreet guys when I was a teen.

Mick cleared his throat, bringing me back to reality. "Will you be joining us for the meeting?" He asked.

"In a few. Mutt and I were just finishing up."

"Okay, we'll be in the conference room." Mick headed out, and Robbie waved at me as he followed, adding a sly smile. I admired his sturdy gate in all his police gear until they disappeared down the hall around the corner.

I turned back around and found Mutt glaring at me. I ignored him and purposely refocused on my work because I didn't want my head clouded any further by distractions of the Robbie kind. "Can you play back that last track for me?"

He pushed some buttons on the control panel. "You know, you've done enough today. Let's wrap up. Besides, I can see in your eyes you want that cop."

I giggled. "Is it that obvious?"

"There was a time *I* tried to hit on you, and you didn't have that twinkle in your eyes."

"And I recall, I told you we'd only ever have a working relationship." I reached for my bag, not arguing with calling it a day.

"Was it the Hawaiian shirt?"

"You mean your uniform of them?" I chuckled. "I don't think I've ever seen you in anything but shorts and brightly colored floral shirts."

"I could change if a woman like you loved me." He crossed his arms and leaned back in the chair. I mirrored him, crossing my arms and parking my rear on the desk of the control panel.

"But that's the thing, Mutt. I respect you and love you just the way you are. Don't you dare change a thing. In fact, I'm going to search for the perfect Hawaiian shirt for you as a gift."

"Okay, deal. How about meeting me for a drink later?"

I laughed as I headed out of the room. "You won't give up, will you?"

"Just a drink between professionals." He followed me out and down the hall.

"Tempting, but no thanks. I've been going to bed early and rising early to jog with Sara lately. Now that she's pregnant, she's slower and I can finally keep up with her."

"Up early? Not out partying at night? Careful, Prima, small town life is changing you."

"No. You know me, I'm a California girl through and through."

"But maybe you see a man like Robbie and it becomes more appealing?"

"Well, he is *nice* to look at." I stopped in my tracks, just outside the conference room, eyeing the lawman inside. "But I'm unsure I can trust my judgment right now with men. Besides, when I pause and think about it, instead of jumping in head first, I realize any man in my life right now would only be a rebound."

"Nothing wrong with rebounds, but yes. Take your time. And if you're really lonely...*I'm* here." He wiggled his eyebrows and elbowed me.

"Oh, Mutt, you're incorrigible. Besides, what would your wife think?" I teased back.

"Nothing, since wife number four took off with half my money and is shacking up with some guy in Peru."

I automatically reached my hand on his arm. "What? Oh, I'm so sorry. I've seen nothing in the entertainment news about your divorce."

"That's because I can't afford one. I had to come out of retirement and get back to work, but it was good timing because Mick started up Wild Horses Music. He has the good business sense like his dad, but without the old man's icy heart."

"I do recall old Mr. Magnus. My first breakout hit record was all because of him, you know. He discovered me, or rather my mom probably slept with him," I snorted.

"Whatever happened, it worked. Lucky you got away from Magnus Music though. They're a total shit show now, run by his son Hugh. He's exactly like his father. An asshole and bastard rolled into one."

I had a good laugh and out of the corner of my eye I saw Robbie, Dillon, and Mick with their heads were bent over a tablet. "I have no idea how Mick came out of that family as good of a person as he is. Without him, I don't know if I'd be here right now."

God, I owed so many people for helping me through what had been the most challenging year of my life.

"Me either. Stick with Mick."

"Yes." I caught Robbie's attention across the room and was lost for a few seconds. Time slowed as his eyes raked down my body.

Mutt snapped his fingers in front of my face. "Earth to Prima."

"Oh, sorry. Guess I should go see what this meeting is about."

"And see that cop?" He nodded into the room.

I blushed and tucked my hair behind my ear. "Maybe. Thanks for everything, Mutt. I'll see you tomorrow in the studio."

"Sure. Whatever. I'll be there—likely with another loud Hawaiian shirt on," he hustled away.

"I'm here, fellas." As I entered the room, all three heads popped up at me, each with grim faces. I dropped my bag off on a chair and approached their huddle. "What's going on?"

Mick held the tablet for me to see. The screen showed a few photos of me at the grocery store I had visited yesterday. I'd worn my Daisy Duke denim shorts and a t-shirt tied at the waist with my hair up in a messy bun and a pair of cowboy boots.

I scoffed at the one showing me bending over to get a box of granola bars from the lowest shelf. "Ugh. Those paparazzi pukes. I don't pay them any attention."

"Not the paps," he said and swiped the screen. "Another note from the stalker. Whoever it is, they're close by."

There on the email, was a photo of a white paper, and handwritten in big bold letters were words that chilled me to the bone: *I SEE THE REAL YOU. YOU CAN'T HIDE FROM ME.*

CHAPTER 5

WANNA TOUCH YOU

ROBBIE

I SAT at the table with the tablet and pored over every email Prima's fan club had received over the past few months. Sara had been in charge of the club for years for her famous twin, and kept meticulous records, making it easy to track these stalker emails from the beginning.

Each one sent anonymously appeared with the same features: a photo of white paper, with block letters in handwriting like a grade schooler. There appeared to be no traceable metadata on the photo.

As if formulaic, they contained a screenshot of some news about her, and then a commentary in writing.

One said, *"Bruce was trash. About time you dumped him."*

Another said, *"Your last film was a rotten tomato. Give up acting. Stick with singing."*

They recently took on a different tone. *"Don't you dare do that concert. Why won't you listen to me? Soon, I'll make you obey."*

"The latest with photos of you taken yesterday prove it's time to take this stalker seriously. I have a few buddies in the cyber crime division up in Louisville I can consult with," I said.

Prima huffed and paced the floor near me with her arms crossed, while Dillon and Mick conferred off to the side.

"The notes seem personal. I wonder if it's someone you're already familiar with? An acquaintance maybe?" I hypothesized. Digging into a new case, like a new mystery, always held the most intrigue for me.

"When you're a celebrity, everyone thinks they know you. They don't, yet they'll believe anything printed online," Prima said. I detected a sad note in her voice. It couldn't be easy being a well-known figure.

"Whoever this is has either followed you here or been right here all along." No way could I imagine anyone in this town would suddenly develop such a fascination for a rock star. Then again, I've dealt with the public for years now and shouldn't be surprised by anything.

"Some sicko. It's no big deal." She stopped pacing at the window and stared out, hugging her sides. I didn't know her well enough yet, but I liked to think I read people well, a skill honed from years as an officer of the peace. And right now, she did a great job acting tough, but I knew underneath there was more to the story.

I stood up and joined her there at the window, a few inches away from her, and was submerged instantly into her fragrance. Like a signature to her personality, it was strong and brassy, but with a hint of sweetness. I'd bet in bed she'd be a tigress one minute and a pussy cat the next.

I shoved away that thought, clearing my throat. "One sick person is all it takes to get close enough to you when you least expect it. Then who knows what they'll do?"

"I know very well what they'll do."

Shit. She did. "Sorry, I didn't mean—"

"It's fine. There's no way I could have predicted the monster my ex would become, taking all my money and ruining my life and career. But my mother holding me hostage this summer? I should have known better, given how she treated Sara and me as we grew up."

It couldn't have been easy for her these past few months, coming to terms with everything she endured. The thing was, no matter the strength she exuded, late at night, when she let her guard down, I'd bet she was still terrified.

The vulnerability in her stance right now took me aback—like a wounded bird who needed tending to. The badge I wore required professionalism, keeping a distance, not crossing the line. The protector in me fought the urge to reach out, hold her tight, help her get through this. I shoved my hands in my pockets.

"I'll need a list of the people close to you, everyone you know. Your mother, the ex, anyone you employ," I said, trying to keep the logical part of my brain functioning amid these wild notions cropping up about her.

"You can't possibly think anyone I know had anything to do with this?"

"I know nothing right now. But I'll feel better when I can eliminate potential culprits, and that starts by looking at everyone you know." I urged her to comply.

"I want surveillance on Prima around the clock," Mick ordered.

"That's hardly necessary, besides I'm not sure I can afford security right now," Prima spat, turning away from the window with her face scrunched up.

"I won't take any chances. We've invested a lot into you and this album."

After sharing a glance with Dillon, I shook my head. "My police department is stretched thin, but I could post a unit outside the studios by day, and at the farm at night."

Since returning to Kissing Springs, with Sara and Charles a couple now, Prima took up residence in the nanny's quarters at Charles' farm. I could imagine it'd piss him off to see a cop car outside his home every night, but he'd have to put up and shut up.

"With the street events in Kissing Springs being a hit and more scheduled, the concerts at the Boyd theater, plus increased celebrity presence, we're thinking of a better solution," Dillon spoke up. "The town shouldn't have to shoulder all our security concerns."

"You know all too well the constant battle I have with my sister over the police department budget and staffing," I said, certain Meadow kept nothing from Dillon about running this town.

"Yes, and toward that end, Mick's come up with a great idea of setting up a security division to support the partnership between my Hot Derby Nights Entertainment Group and his Wild Horses Music."

"We'll call it the Knights Security Team. A group of men and women hand-picked to provide security as needed, wherever needed." Mick finished proudly.

They eagerly awaited my approval of the idea, but I hesitated with some immediate reservations. "I guess I can't stop you from getting this idea off the ground. I'll need some assurances there will be constant communication between my officers and these...these..."

"Knights." Dillon provided. "And of course. I wouldn't expect anything less. In fact, I wouldn't do this unless you were one hundred percent on board with the idea, Robbie."

All eyes stared at me, even Prima's. The past year in Kissing Springs had been like no other, but it's what Meadow wanted. When the town voted her in as mayor, she called for change in the region and that's what we got. With the townsfolk rallying behind her, it'd been a fast and furious year from the start.

New businesses cropped up, people were moving back, and these celebrity tours Dillon and Mick were bringing in meant more out of towners visiting for the concerts. My officers could hardly keep up with all the demands, between traffic, brawls at bars, and more.

All this growth was a good thing for the survival of Kissing Springs. But it called for a bigger police presence, perhaps led by someone tougher than me with more experience in larger departments. I only ever wanted to lead my small-town police force. Was I cut out for anything bigger?

"The Knights, huh? Unless the mayor lets me staff another ten officers, I don't see how I can turn down the idea." I gave in.

Dillon's smile reflected relief. "Wonderful. In fact, I already have someone in mind to lead this. You remember Andrew Stockey? He's been helping manage the dancers at Derby Nights, but he'd be great at managing the Knights for us, what with his military background and all."

"How quickly can this get up and running, Dillon? I want Prima guarded now," Mick demanded again. From the moment I met him this summer, he came across as down to earth, and a good guy, constantly talking about his wife and kids. In business, he knew his stuff, so I couldn't fault him for protecting his assets.

"Really, you guys are fretting over nothing," Prima finally spoke up, and strutted over to her bag. She shouldered it, shaking her head. "Trust me. This stalker will go away. Now, I'm going home. I have better things to do with my time."

"Prima, please, keep a low profile for now." Mick begged.

"I'm done here. You boys figure it out." She waved us off with her hand in the air, giving a slightly dramatic exit. I hid a smile; I wouldn't expect anything less from a celebrity.

I ran out after her. "Hey, hold up."

She sighed and pressed the down arrow at the elevator. Twirling on her heels, she faced me and leaned on the elevator door.

"What do you want, Robbie? Do you have more warnings about how I should be careful? Or you want to remind me to keep my pepper spray handy? Or a half dozen other tips you think will help in case I come face to face with a stupid stalker?"

"No, actually, I was simply going to tell you I admire your spunk. You are fierce, darling. I'll give you that." I threw my smoldering smile at her, in case it would help.

"Oh." She pinked—Hell yes. I, Robbie Boyd, made this great rock star blush, and oh, it looked so good on her. Images suddenly came to mind of a dozen other ways I could produce a similar outcome if we ever happened to be alone.

"Just do a favor for me?" I leaned my palm high on the frame surrounding the door. We stood close, igniting all kinds of devilish thoughts in my brain.

Her breath hitched, and her lashes fluttered. "Like what?"

Fuck, I didn't know what got into me, but I reached up and tucked a stray lock behind her ear. "I'd hate for anything to happen to you. Be vigilant of your surroundings, please? You have an album to finish and I cannot wait to hear it."

"Well, just for you, since you asked nicely. I'll be careful." For a few seconds, our breaths entwined and our eyes heated with a connection so intense words weren't necessary.

This close, inside the depths of her blues, I lost myself and my reason for being here. I wanted to touch more of her, until the elevator door dinged and opened behind her. She backed in, never taking her eyes off of mine. We eye fucked each other good and hot until the door closing separated us.

"Wow." I swallowed hard, adjusted myself, and had to recite the ABCs before I could calm my cock down enough to face Dillon and Mick in the conference room again.

What the hell was it about her that made me lose all sensibility? Was it a fuck I needed, having denied myself female companionship for too long?

One thing was for certain. Prima had to be off limits. I was the head of police around here, and I needed to keep my head on straight. I had one job when it came to her: Keep her safe. There's no way in hell she would get harmed while in Kissing Springs.

CHAPTER 6

I GOT YOU, SISTER

PRIMA

STRESS WAS a bitch and right now, I had my fill of it, ready to kick it to the curb. I woke up stiff all over. Restful sleep had been scarce for the past week, with too many thoughts swarming through my head all at once.

Would my album be well received by critics?

How would my fans take my divorce concert?

When would I stop tossing and turning, worried about everything—and dredging up the past?

I thought I'd worked through my emotions and the shock of what happened this summer, but things were still simmering under the surface. Like I checked the lock on my door at least ten times throughout the night, an irritating habit I'd formed since Mom did a number on me.

While dealing with my divorce this past summer, and feeling at my lowest, I'd given in to her urgings for a visit. I thought maybe Lucy could console me, to be a decent mother, for once, but how wrong I was.

It was incredulous that she actually drugged me and kept me locked in a room, all intending to take over managing my career. What the hell? How on fucking earth could a mother do that to their child?

I should have known her money-hungry ways would possess her and turn her into a monster.

It took everything I had to escape from her one night. The humbling experience—to go from having it all to having to beg Sara and friends to help me—was something I never wanted to go through again.

While I'd worked some of this out at a retreat center before returning to Kissing Springs, the therapy wasn't a total cure. I still had demons to work through. A chill ran down my spine even now, at the sink brushing my teeth, as I thought about that horrible ordeal.

After spending most of the night tossing and turning, I was in no mood for my usual morning jog with Sara. When I walked into the kitchen at Charles' farmhouse, she hardly looked ready, either. With pale skin and tired eyes, she munched on saltine crackers with a glass of water nearby.

"Hey, little mama," I greeted her warmly with a bright smile, so good at hiding all my problems away. "Those babies in your belly making you sick?"

"Hm-hmm. I'll be fine. Just give me a minute," she said through a mouthful.

"Such a warrior you are. You know, we could skip out on the jog this morning."

"No. I'll be fine. I just had a rough night of sleep."

"You too? I thought now that your world is perfect, nothing would bring you down." I poured a glass of water and leaned against the counter across from her.

"Far from perfect. Actually, I want to talk with you about something." She set aside the crackers, giving me that serious look she used when it was something important, only this time, it was different, with her hand caressing her slight baby bump.

"I know I've worked for years managing your fan club and communication, but...I'd like to step aside. Now that you're back to working on an album, I'm sure you'll have number one hits, go out on tour, and money will flow again. Just with the babies coming—"

"Say no more." I interrupted her. "I got you, sister. You have your own world now. No room for me."

"Prim, of course I have room for *you*. But with my work at Wild Horses Music and, let's face it, I'm an instant mom now to Charles' twins, and with two more on the way...God, I hope I'll be able to handle it all." A tear streaked out of one corner of her eye.

"Oh, come here." I hugged her tight. "You're going to be fine. Of the two of us, I think you were born to be a mother."

She laughed as we separated and dabbed her eyes. "Anything has to be better than Lucy."

"Is that what you fear? Being a horrible mother like ours? Trust me, you won't be. I know you'll work hard at being a loving, caring mom. Look how you are with Grace and Hope."

"You're right." Charles' kids took to Sara fast. I couldn't blame them. My sister was the best.

"Of course I am. Besides, if you ever turn out like Lucy, I'll kick your ass."

"Please do." We laughed, and this was good. We'd come a long way through so much together, and nothing would ever break our bond.

"Tell you what, I'd be happy if we forgot about exercise this morning and just had a pumpkin spice latte from that place, Minnie's Pie Shop, on Main Street," I suggested. "I overheard some women at the studio saying how good they are, all thick and creamy, and the pumpkin scones are supposed to be—"

Suddenly, Sara heaved into the sink at the mention of these autumn treats. I looked away. "Ew. Guess not, huh?"

After rinsing her mouth out with tap water, she shook her head. "I wondered when morning sickness would hit me. I've felt so incredible—until now."

"Let's go for an easy stroll downtown." I felt silly saying Kissing Springs had a downtown when it was one street that ran for only a few blocks and not a skyscraper in sight. But I learned recently how the locals referred to Main Street as *going downtown*. "Then after, we'll get breakfast at the pie shop and hope you'll keep it down."

"Did someone say pie?" Charles walked into the kitchen, shirtless and in a pair of sweats. The man had a six-pack that was very pleasing to the eye, but he belonged to Sara and very much off the market, being the father of twin girls with another set of twins on the way. "If you're going to Minnie's, could you pick up a Bourbon Pumpkin Pie? If memory serves, she makes this sweet pecan crumble with caramel drizzle on top. So good, almost better than sex."

"Puh-lease put a shirt on, Charlie, and don't mention sex in front of me," I grumbled. The last thing I needed was to ogle my future brother-in-law.

He looked about to retort, but then Sara heaved over the sink once again. To his credit, he ignored me and reached for her, holding her hair and rubbing her back. "Our babies are doing a number on you today, aren't they, sweetheart? What can I do to make it better for you?"

"Quit talking about pump...pump...bleb." She dry heaved. Clearly, she would not survive this fall season and all the pumpkin spiced treats.

"I'll buy you ginger gum. And acupuncture is supposed to help, so I could fly in my old acupuncturist from Chicago?" Worry set in his voice.

After rinsing with water again, she entered his embrace, resting her cheek on his chest. She fit under his chin now, but eventually, when her stomach grew with two babies in it and got in the way, she wouldn't.

I eyed them, holding each other, his lips kissing the top of her head. Such a sweet scene. Charles could be a tough bosshole in business, but this side of him, holding my sister, was endearing, and I knew the man loved my sister completely. I couldn't be happier for her, and he had better treat her like a queen or I'd raise hell.

Then a pang hit my heart, something new, something painful. I was—jealous?

"Could you buy more saltines?" Sara croaked.

"Anything for you, baby." They locked lips in front of me. I looked away, my eyes landing on the fridge where a school calendar was held up by a magnet, and a dozen other magnets showed off Grace and Hope's artwork, mainly scribbles.

Everything here was so real, so homey, so big-happy-family. Exactly what Sara wanted.

Could I see myself someday in a similar situation with a family and a man of my own? What the hell did I want now that I was a free woman? Suddenly, it was like the walls were closing in on me, feeling trapped again, like I was when Lucy locked me away.

"Come on. Back to bed with me. The girls won't wake up for another hour. You can rest in my arms." Charles said, and led Sara out of the kitchen, but he grabbed the cracker package last minute to take with them.

"I hope you'll feel better, Sara," I called after them. "Don't worry about me, I'll..."

My words died off as they disappeared down the hall. She had him, and she'd be fine. But would I? I had no one, and the realization that I might end up in this world all alone almost had *me* running to the sink to throw up. My pulse sped and my vision clouded.

One thing was for sure, I needed out of here, and to fight through whatever was bringing me down.

CHAPTER 7

GIVE ME A REASON TO FALL

PRIMA

SARA'S MORNING sickness wouldn't deter me from enjoying the sights and tastes of the season. I showered, forgoing exercise, and opted instead for a latte at Minnie's.

I had a full day of recording ahead on one of my toughest songs for my vocal range, not to mention the song Mutt disliked the most after receiving the band recordings from Nashville yesterday. Already, I knew, we'd probably butt heads over it, but coffee first.

I entered the quaint pie shop, immediately consumed by the fragrances of fresh apple pie and other homemade varieties. With its decor of yellow checkered tablecloths, pumpkins and gourds grouped in baskets here and there, and garlands of fall leaves, all done tastefully, I had to hand it to the owners for capturing the signatures of the season.

My mood lightened more seeing Robbie standing and talking to a woman behind the counter. As usual, in full uniform, he wore the look of a protector nicely. Another lifetime, another place, I'd love to see what he packed under all the protective gear he wore.

"Hi. Fancy running into you here," I said with a grin, looking up into his eyes. I very much admired his tall build, and probably so did every woman who came within five feet of him.

"I always make my way here in the mornings to check on my aunt and uncle. Prima, this is my Aunt Minnie." He introduced us.

The mature woman looked me up and down above her half-rimmed glasses. "Well, aren't you lovely? It isn't often we get a bona fide star visiting. And don't let Robbie fool you. He stops by every day for free food," she said, winking at me.

I liked her already. A pencil holding her gray hair up in a bun, bright pink lipstick slathered on, and a cardigan sweater over her white apron only enhanced her cheerful nature.

"If you wouldn't make the best damn cinnamon rolls, I wouldn't have to stop by and eat them." He kissed her forehead. "You should try them, Prima. They're out of this world."

"Oh, no. Maybe some other time. I have a red dress to fit into in a few weeks, remember? I just stopped in for a pumpkin spiced latte before heading to the studio." The sound of bells on the door announced the arrival of more customers behind me.

"Robbie will make it for you, and it's on the house," Minnie said, and grabbed a few menus on her way to greet the patrons.

"That's unnecessary. I'm happy to pay—" She was off before I could resist.

"Will that be for here or to go? And if you say it's for here, you can join me in that booth over there and we can talk for a few minutes before you rush off to make your next number one hit." He winked, and I didn't mind. Gotta love a family of winkers.

I chuckled. "Well, no one ever accused me of letting a fan down. I'll have it here." Robbie worked behind the counter, making my drink, and I observed his every move. Steady. Sturdy. Strong. "So you're a barista *and* the sheriff?"

"What can I say? I'm very talented at a lot of things, but I'm not a sheriff. Just the chief." His sly grin was so fucking sexy.

"Is there a difference?"

"Yup." He put my cup on a saucer and expertly swirled the silky foam on top, then used a stick to form a pattern of hearts through it. "I don't know many sheriffs who can make a latte *this* damn good. Come on."

Swoon. My mouth hung open as I followed behind him while he somehow carried both our drinks plus a plated cinnamon roll over to a booth. On the entire walk, my eyes roamed his broad back and toned ass. I never knew I could be so attracted to a man in uniform, but it was there...

something between us. From the first moment we'd met, it was always unsaid, lingering, teasing, daring for something more to happen.

Prior to my marriage, I'd have gobbled Robbie up like he was my next meal. Of course, every man eventually found some way to use me, and Bruce was the worst. The humiliation of the way he treated me, tore me down, and stole all of my money still stings. Would there ever be a time when it wouldn't?

Now, post-divorce, how do I trust my choices in men? It made jumping into my next relationship more challenging than anything. My wounded heart would take some time to heal, and I'd need to give myself some grace.

As we sat in the booth by the window, though, I centered myself in front of Robbie. Big mistake because the entire time, I took in his wavy brown hair and bold blue eyes, the crinkles in the corners when he laughed, and the sexy way he grinned at everything I said.

Our discussion flowed as we chatted about what it's like to be on tour with a rock and roll band. He made me laugh with his questions and comments, and he seemed to hang on every word of mine, like any fan would. Or maybe like each word was laced in gold—as in, did he see me as a quick way to beef up his bank account if we got close? I shook the thought away.

Robbie couldn't possibly be a bad guy out to take advantage of me. He's far from the likes of my ex, plus he's a cop, for Christ's sake. But still...I doubted myself too much.

"I recall the first concert of yours I went to," he started.

"Oh? How many have you seen?"

He grinned. "A few. But the first one was the best."

Oof. He blushed. Nice—No, not nice. He's just a fan, fans crush on me all the time. It means nothing.

"Yeah, my buddy Kipp was getting married about several years ago, the first among my friends to do so. At the time, your *Heartbreak-Her* album was hot, number one on the charts, and the same weekend we planned to fly off to Vegas for his bachelor party, you were performing there. We all splurged and got front row tickets."

"No. Seriously? You were that close to me?" I wondered if I saw him, if anything registered while I was singing, and noticed how handsome he was. But on stage, I was always immersed in Prima, the performer, giving the fans more than they paid for, with no room to think of anything else.

"You probably don't remember, but there was a point, late in the concert, where you took your bra off and flung it at me."

"I did?" My eyes bulged. "Yeah, I have a point late in every concert where I'm dripping with sweat. The heat of the lights, the physical exertion, and the adrenaline get to be too much. If I could be naked on stage at that point, I would. Do...you still have this bra?"

He chuckled, and his gaze drew me in. "Maybe. Tucked away in a drawer somewhere with all my prized possessions."

God, what would being his possession feel like? He's perfectly tempting. Practically sitting here giving me every reason to fall for him.

My phone vibrated with an incoming call and jerked me out of my thoughts. "Oh, it's Mutt. I'm late and need to get to the studio. The latte was lovely, but I—"

"Need another to go?" He'd have probably jumped and whipped up a second one for me if I nodded my head. He's possibly that good of a guy.

"No, I need to head out. Tough day ahead at the studio." I stood and gathered my things.

"You haven't eaten anything. Here, at least take the last quarter of my roll, I insist."

"Do you know what that would do to my waistline? My seamstress is already pitching a fit, trying to get my costumes perfect for the concert."

He cocked his head and with a twinkle in his eyes they roamed down my chest and back up. His tongue darted out wetting the center of his lips before he said, "I think you've more than earned your rightful place among the rock gods and should be a woman allowed to eat anything she wants— as long as it pleases her."

Oh God, why did he have to say that and look so edible himself? If I could escape this impromptu meet up without soaking my panties, it'd be a miracle.

Chapter 8

Kiss Me Like That Deadly

Robbie

"I came as soon as I got the call. Where is it?" I barged into Dillon's conference room late in the afternoon, where he, Meadow, Andrew, and Sara stood in front of another email from the stalker projected on the big screen.

A photo was enlarged there, and my jaw hit the floor. It showed Prima and me this morning, sitting in the booth at the window, chatting and laughing at Minnie's. Someone took it from somewhere outside, spying on us.

In the same type of email as before, the words read: *WHORE. DON'T YOU KNOW YOU'RE MINE? YOU WILL SOON ENOUGH.*

"Shit. Did Prima see this yet?" My eyebrows stitched together.

"I called her. She's pissed," Sara said.

"Is she coming over?"

"No. She got into a fight with Mutt over creative differences and just needs to be alone for a while."

I stared at the photo again, trying to study the angle and location someone could have possibly taken it from. Upset at myself, I was supposed to be protecting her.

Instead, I got caught up with her laugh, and with the sparkle in her eyes as she talked about her life on the road as a rock star. She was so damned alluring, sharing that part of herself with me.

This was why I didn't get too emotionally involved in cases —and I broke that rule without even trying. When I should have been watching for any signs of a stalker, I showed her off, front and center by the window, unaware of how I was luring the stalker in.

"I called Dallas, the Knight on duty earlier today guarding Prima, and asked if he could recall anyone suspicious hanging about or taking photos," Andrew spoke up. As the head of the new Knight's Security Team, he was to keep a man on Prima night and day.

"And?"

"He said he was front and center across the street from you the entire time, and recalled nothing out of the ordinary. Except he was pretty hyped that Mutt walked up to him for a chat. Dallas, being an avid rock enthusiast, recognized the producer right away and even got his autograph."

I smirked at him. "Do you have a man on her now? Where is she?"

"Yes, Foster has this shift. Let me check." He tapped into his phone. While waiting, I stared at the recent note and photo, removing my Louisville Sluggers ball cap and scrubbing a hand through my hair. I was dressed casually, set to meet up with friends for dinner at Lockland Distillery tonight, celebrating Kipp and Tracy's anniversary, some of my best friends since grade school.

"Oh no," Andrew groaned. "Foster said he lost her once she left the studio. He drove to the Montgomery farm and didn't see her car there yet, either."

"Clearly, we need more training for the Knights in how to tail your mark." I scowled and rushed out of the room. While I believed Dillon was right, that Andrew was the man for the job, obviously, we still had work to do.

Once I scrambled into my SUV, I took off and drove around, looking for any signs of her. It was a small town, and it shouldn't take long to find her and that sporty red rental car she had.

I drove up and down Main Street, and connected side streets, checked out all the restaurants and distilleries, even eyed the walkway along the springs.

Eventually, Andrew called me. "Hey, it turns out, Foster hadn't realized she'd parked her car in Charles' garage."

"The fuck?" I rolled my eyes. "Tell him to knock on the door and make sure she's there."

"He did."

"And?"

"He got an earful from Prima about how she didn't need to be babysat and he could go fuck himself."

"Yep, sounds like a diva." Part of me was amused by her reaction, the other part was pissed. There's a stalker on the loose nearby, and she didn't seem to take it seriously enough.

"I apologize, sir, about all of this. Any change to the assignment?"

I liked the guy, and I was certain, eventually, the Knights would have their shit together. This was a new endeavor, and we'd work the kinks out. "No. Keep watch. Thanks."

By the time I arrived at the Skeleton Bar at Lockland's, I'd missed the dinner. My mood could have shot the moon down, so it was better anyway.

Some jerk off taking photos of me and Prima didn't sit well with me at all, but seeing Kipp and his wife, Tracy, so happy brought me back a little. So did a Double Old Fashioned, meeting my quota for one drink tonight, considering I drove here.

Being the chief of police came with tremendous responsibilities to the community. If I ever felt the need for a bender, I didn't drive. Period. I didn't need the old biddies talking about me being a drunk around town; it was bad enough they kept tabs on the lack of any females in my life.

I looked around at my friends, some I worked with in various capacities, some I'd known since school days, all of them I wouldn't trade for the world. I loved my small town life; without a doubt, this was where I belonged. Still, it was like the high school kid in me ran away with all the fantasies of being with a rock star...all the way to Hollywood, where I definitely didn't belong.

Kipp and his cousin, Blake Wilson, joined me at the bar, ordering the same drink. Lockland's bourbon was known for its warm notes of spices and fruits, but right now, it was the only thing taking the edge off.

I finished a sip as Blake slapped my back. "How's it going, chief?"

"I'd say he's doing fine," Kipp answered before I could, chuckling and slightly slurring his words. "Considering all the rumors about him and a certain rock goddess who has graced Kissing Springs with her presence. Some old biddy saw you two this morning at Minnie's and it's all the town's talking about. Hell, the news reached my fire station before noon. That has to be a record."

"Prima fucking diva. Wow! Isn't she newly divorced? She's probably looking for a rebound man. Wouldn't that give new meaning to Kissing Springs as the romance capital if she found the lucky bastard here?" As Blake laughed, his pecs jiggled.

We all kept in good shape, being first responders, always ready for action. Kipp headed up the Kissing Springs firehouse, and Blake worked at Search and Rescue for the county. It was a toss up between the three of us which one could bench more, a little healthy competition that carried over from high school to this day.

Blake continued. "Why, if I wasn't so busy, I'd come down here to give it my best shot with her. Why not? I'll bet she's a handful in bed."

He was often out on the trails and in the hills, so I had little to worry about seeing him and Prima together. Besides, she wasn't anything to me; she could fuck who she wanted. So why did my grip on my glass almost crush it?

"Knock it off. She's been through a lot. The last thing she needs is a rebound." My gruff voice had their eyebrows hitting their hairlines.

"Dang, someone's got your back up and stars in your eyes. Come on, you know we're teasing," Kipp chuckled.

"Yup. Clearly, your response says *Back off. She's mine.* I respect that. Just be careful, buddy. She looks like she's a little heartbreaker." Blake winked, then turned his attention to the redhead taking up the barstool next to him. "Hey, how are you doing? I'm Blake."

I shook my head at his playboy ways. He and I broke up with our exes about the same time. The only difference was he got right back out there, playing the field, hardly taking time to assess things. Unlike me, who took a few years to figure myself out. But besides Kipp, Blake had been a lifelong friend, and another good guy I could trust to always have my back.

I hadn't been that interested in dating—until now. Prima seemed to have ignited some kind of spark. My mind raced with possibilities, wondering if I really should get back out there and date.

"Really, dude, are you okay?" Kipp asked. "You have a thing for this woman? You know I can keep a secret, and even the old biddies bribing me with their best southern barbecued ribs wouldn't coax it out of me." Kipp's been there for me more times than I could count.

When I had a bad case and needed to talk through the evidence, when I broke up with my ex—when I couldn't find her sister, a cold case that haunts me to this day—he'd always been there like a brother to me.

"I don't know. There's a certain chemistry between me and Prima—damn, it's strong. Each time I see her, the more time I want with her. It's beginning to blur the lines."

"Hell, blur them fuckers," Kipp elbowed me. "You need to do something, man. I'm tired of seeing my best friend alone."

I snorted and ignored that. "I'm trying to keep professional, but it doesn't help that some jerk off is stalking her."

"No shit? Well, no matter the romantic situation, if she's got you watching over her, she'll be safe. If you need any help in finding whoever is behind it, you know Blake and I are here for you."

I nodded and finished my drink, thankful for them. Behind Kipp's back, I noticed his wife, Tracy, walking over with her sister, Jayne. "Hey, congrats, by the way, on your anniversary. Ten years is pretty amazing. What's your advice for keeping a woman happy so long?"

"Eat her pussy, man. Every night. That's the secret." He winked, with no idea that his wife was standing right there.

She crossed her arms and cleared her throat to get his attention. "That's your secret? Don't let him fool you, Robbie. Communication is key. Or how about drawing a bath for me and taking care of the kids for a while so I can have some me-time?"

He laughed and caught her up in an embrace that took her feet off the floor. "Yes, all the above. Now my secrets to a happy marriage are all out on the table."

"Hey there, Robbie," Tracy hugged me after he put her down. "I'm so glad you made it tonight. And you're just in time."

"For what?" I asked.

"Kipp promised me a dance tonight for our anniversary. So we're headed to the Boot Scoot. You're coming with us, and I won't take no for an answer."

Kipp rolled his eyes, not exactly known to be a guy who liked to dance or had any moves on the floor. "I think I said *maybe* we would, which is far from a promise."

"Uh-huh. You're dancing with me or you'll sleep on the couch."

"Good thing our couch is comfy." He joked, and she slapped his arm. Before she could retort, he hauled her over his shoulder and yelled, "Come on, everyone, I promised my wife a dance. So if you wanna join us at the Boot Scoot, y'all can laugh at me."

"You're coming, too, chief," Jayne said, and linked elbows with me, hauling me off the barstool. I noticed the ring on her finger. She had been working for Dillon over the past year, and recently made it public knowledge of how she and Andrew were engaged.

"Fine." I grumbled.

"So this new Knights Security team is keeping Andrew busy. I hope it does well," she said as we made our way out to the parking lot.

"He's doing all right. With a little more training, I think it could be a top-notch organization."

She faced me a few feet away from my SUV. "I've known you for a long time, so I hope you don't mind me asking this. Will you watch after him, please? I don't know what I would do if-if..."

I knew the terrified look in her eyes. I'd seen it before in the wives and husbands of my officers. The risks we all took serving and protecting the public each day were many.

Not known for taking things lightly or half-assed, I knew I'd watch over the Knights team as well, like they were an extension of my small-town police unit. "Don't worry. I'll do all I can for him. You just keep loving him and keeping him happy at home."

Anxiety swept away off her face replaced by a grin. "Thanks, chief." She hugged me, then jogged off to join her sister in their car.

I didn't much feel like partying, but I also knew myself and the mood I was in. I'd go home and think about Prima, and stew over the stalker case all night long, so I was better off being around people and keeping my mind occupied for a while.

Only the second we stepped into the crowded bar, with more people than I'd ever seen packed into it, my eyes landed on the rock goddess, singing with the house band on stage.

My feet plowed forward before my brain kicked in, pushing through the crowd and making it right up to the edge of the stage. For someone who was supposed to be lying low, she obviously needed schooling on what exactly that meant.

She got the crowd going with her vocals, singing Sweet Home Alabama. The loud music practically vibrated the nails out of the old wooden floor. My head bopped to the riffs; I couldn't help it, but I forced a stern gaze and crossed my arms over my chest.

The showman in her knew exactly how to work the crowd. At one point, she ripped open the flannel shirt she had on; the buttons flew everywhere. She flung it out into the crowd and continued singing. My eyes glued to her chest. Her black bra under a tight white tank top couldn't prevent her nipples from appearing.

Then she spotted me. With a coy smile, she danced over plopped her ass down on the stage, laid back, and let her head dangle off of it in front of me, all while finishing singing the chorus into the mic.

Fuck, she was a sight, but I should carry her outside right now and end this before anyone gets hurt, including my heart.

Before I could move, she reached up and pulled me down by my neck. Our lips crashed in an upside down kiss. She captured my bottom lip, sucking it in and teasing her tongue along it.

Hands down, it had to be the most sexy and deadly kiss I'd ever been the recipient of. Wild horses couldn't pull me away as the surrounding crowd blurred, and she took liberties with me.

I sucked back, capturing her lips and growling, though we were probably the only two to hear it. My hands begged to roam, to palm her nipples, to reach further down her torso and dig under the band of her tight jeans.

A disruption in the crowd and people slamming into me from behind interrupted things.

She laughed and stood back up, but then she narrowly dodged a beer bottle whizzing past her face. It bashed into the drum set behind her. The band cut the music, and I stood on my toes to peer out across the crowd and see where it came from. All hell broke loose with a fight somewhere in the sea of people.

"Fuck this." I wasn't taking any chances. I jumped on the stage, hauled her over my shoulder and carried her out the back door behind the building.

CHAPTER 9

GONNA BE YOU RESCUING ME

PRIMA

"PUT ME DOWN!" I screamed, pounding against Robbie's ass with my fists. When he set my feet on the ground in the middle of the parking lot, I hid the fact that I had a little buzz going and attempted to control my swaying.

"Christ, I'm trying to save you from those idiots in there. If that bottle had hit your head—"

"Yeah, well, it didn't. And don't think for a minute that was my first bar fight. I've probably seen more action in podunk town bars in my lifetime than you have." My fists were tight at my sides and I glared up at him.

"Okay, yeah. You're right, tough girl. I forgot you were trained by the School of Rockology to manage a lunatic whose every intention is to hurt you on stage or off."

I didn't like his sarcastic tone one bit, but damn, I loved kissing those full lips of his. "Don't talk to me like that. I know what I'm doing." I headed back toward the bar, but he caught my arm and swung me around to face him.

"Like how you're lying low, singing in front of a hundred people in a crowded bar when there's a stalker on the loose? You call this keeping a low profile in town?"

"I call this living my life. Not cowering in a corner."

"Guess that's rock and roll for you. Living on the edge."

"I don't know any other way." I yanked my arm away from him and stomped on his foot with the heel of my boot.

"Ow. What the fuck?" He yelped and doubled over. I ran to my car, dug the keys from my pocket, and hit the button to unlock the doors.

I launched myself into the driver's seat, but his big hand prevented me from closing the door. Tears threatened my eyes, but in no way would I show him. "Let me go."

"You're not getting away."

"Yes, I am. I'm leaving this town. Driving anywhere and getting away from everything."

"No. You're not driving when all four of your tires have been slashed." He pointed at my back tire.

"What?" I climbed back out and sure enough, it was flat. I ran around the entire car eyeballing each one, then ended up back in front of him. A stupid tear rolled down my cheek, and I angrily swiped it away. "Who could have done this?"

"My guess is the stalker. *Now* will you take this a little more seriously?"

A nearby crack like a stick breaking underneath a foot snapped him to attention. He turned his back to me, caging me in between the door, my car, and him, as if he was my armor. Only then did I realize that he somehow had produced a gun and was pointing it down at the ground with both hands gripping it, at the ready, as he scanned the parking lot, on the lookout in case whoever did this was still nearby.

The hairs on the back of my neck stood on end. In the dark like this, could a mad person be watching us? A freak who was obsessed with me and meant me harm? The reality of it all hit hard and swept me up into emotions I could no longer contain. Robbie was right; I wasn't as tough as I acted.

"Sir, you got her?" I jumped at the man rushing up to us. My hands automatically went to Robbie's waist as if I knew, deep down, he'd protect me.

"Yeah, Andrew. Her tires are slashed, though."

"Shit. I was pinned in by the melee inside, and I couldn't get to her fast enough. This is getting serious now."

I peered around Robbie's big frame to see the man he was talking to, but gasped when the door to the bar opened and the fight spilled outside. Men were pushing and shoving each other, shouting obscenities. Women were as bad, or worse. Sirens blared, coming closer and cop cars pulled into the lot.

"My men have arrived. Sweep the parking lot and stick around to help them sort things out. I'm taking her with me, and I'll text you the address. Have one of your guys post there overnight and keep watch. I'll check in with you in the morning," Robbie ordered with a strict, all-business tone.

"You got it." Andrew jogged off toward the nearest police vehicle.

"I don't need to be babysat by the Knights," my voice wavered. I fumed, crossing my arms with one last show of what remained of my bravery, but it was all a facade and I knew it.

Robbie flipped back to me. "I don't care what the fuck you say. We're not staying here to see how this plays out. My job is to keep you safe, darling, and that's what I'll do."

Suddenly, he hauled me over his shoulder again, and this time I didn't fight it as he rushed across the parking lot. Wherever he was taking me didn't matter, as long as it was with him. Somehow I knew—I trusted—he would do exactly what he was supposed to and protect me.

In a black SUV, he set me down in the passenger seat. I kept my head low, so my hair would hide my face. I didn't want him to see how truly terrified I was, but it was no use. With a finger, he gently lifted my chin.

"I'm sorry if I was rough. I didn't mean to scare you. But if anything happened to you...I couldn't live with that." His voice soothed, as if he'd flipped a switch. The tough lawman showed a softer side, wiping away a few of my tears. In his eyes, dark blue and so true in the moonlight, how could I doubt his intentions?

"Need anything, chief?" A male voice called out behind us. I gasped and jumped again, my hand holding my heart.

"It's okay. It's just one of my officers," he reassured me. "Nah, Brax. Text me when you get all this under control. And call Ty to tow that red Mercedes over there to our lot. Have it dusted for prints."

"Sure thing." The sound of footsteps jogging away indicated we were alone in the vehicle again.

"Here." Robbie reached behind the seat and produced a sweatshirt. "Put this on. You look cold." He bunched it up, and I ducked into it and put my arms in. The gray sweatshirt with KSPD in bold blue letters instantly warmed me and smelled like him, like a promise of security and sanctuary.

I imagined it might be as good as being in his arms. In the small space, our eyes connected and I almost thought he'd kiss me, but then he reached over and buckled me in.

"Where are we going?" I asked, my voice husky and hoarse. Between a rough day at the studio with Mutt, almost getting into a yelling match with him over creative differences with my song, then singing my heart out at the bar, and dealing with Robbie, it was too much. I long ago learned how to take proper care of my throat—my most precious gift—and today I abused it.

"My place."

"Already, on our first date?" I deadpanned. It worked, too, and his chuckle broke the tension.

"That's good. Keep your humor through this and you'll be all right." He ran around to the driver's side. We took off, leaving a mess of people and police behind us, but we hardly talked as he received call after call from his guys through a special radio in his car.

I listened to Robbie continuing to give orders and admired his ability to be cool under pressure. I overheard that the guys who'd started trouble were some cousins of Charles and Dillon.

The way Robbie reacted, I figured he must not be a big fan of the Montgomerys. He muttered something about history there, and I made a note to ask him about it sometime, considering my sister was about to marry one of them.

I watched outside the window as we wound through the dark streets of Kissing Springs. All the pretty old homes were lit up at night and so picturesque, each one unique compared to Southern California, where houses were often cookie cutters of each other. Eventually, he parked in front of a little white house located behind a bed-and-breakfast.

"You live here?"

"Yep. Hope this is okay? Meadow and I own the BNB, but she's too busy to deal with it. I rent it out on the side and take care of it in my spare time, and I live here in the back. It's not much, just a little one-bedroom cottage. You can have the bed and I'll take the couch."

"I could call Sara and have them come get me."

His jaw tightened. "I'm sure Charles would do his best to protect you for Sara's sake, but other than locking you in my jail cell, the only place I'm *certain* you'll be safe, darling, is right here under the same roof with me."

"Well, when the sheriff makes a demand like that, how can I resist?"

"I'm not a sheriff," he chuckled and shook his head. "I was hired as the chief to oversee police operations in this *town*. Sheriff Woolsy holds an elected position and oversees the entire county. Understand the difference?"

"Sure...chief." I peered at him through my lashes with a weak smile. The night wore me down, and I stifled a yawn.

"You look like you could use a bed."

"I could use something. But yes, a bed, for starters, maybe a drink."

"Whatever you want. I'll try to make your night as comfortable as possible." He nodded. "Come on. Let's get you inside."

Whatever I wanted...I wanted a lot of things. I wanted it all, and why shouldn't I expect the best life could offer after everything I'd been through?

Robbie ran around to my side and opened my door, holding out his hand to help me out. I took it, shocked by the warmth I found there. His heat radiated throughout my body, like a force field, and finally I trusted it would be him rescuing me from now on.

Our joined hands linked us for only a moment and solidified one thing. Right now, all I wanted was to explore the connection I seemed to have with my small town protector.

CHAPTER 10

CRAZY ABOUT YOU

PRIMA

AFTER A TOUR of Robbie's cottage that lasted all of thirty seconds, I found the place neat and tidy. Was he anal compulsive about cleanliness, or did he have female help?

"Can I have something to drink?" I cleared my throat from my voice sounding rough.

From the fridge, he produced a bottle of water and handed it over. "This do for now? Wait here. I need to lock up my gun." He left the kitchen, and I chugged at least half of it down by the time he returned.

I mulled about noticing his things while he fielded more texts and calls from his officers. A small brown leather couch and club chair took up most of the room, and the big screen

TV hung on one wall. Hardly typical cottage decor, but very manly.

A row of built-in shelves under the TV held a variety of memorabilia, books, old records, and a turntable. The trophies caught my eye first, sitting there in marble and bronze needing a little dusting—basketball and football MVP awards, a few championship years, and one for a record of some sort. That accounted for some of his athletic build and clearly proved a competitive side.

The books were all mysteries and thrillers, police procedure manuals, and some self-help books here and there. Interesting. From the next shelf, I pulled a few of the albums out part way to see what each one was, and approved of his choices: Led Zeppelin, the Beatles, the Stones, plenty of other rock albums spanning a few decades...and every album of mine.

A grin broadened across my face seeing those. Robbie wasn't kidding when he said he was a fan of mine. I'd never been with a fan, come to think of it, not anyone outside of the music business ever. Like a lightbulb switching on over my head, I realized the very heart of my mistakes with men over the years.

In the music business, everyone was dog eat dog, backstabbing, hustling to get to the top. It soiled my mother in her pursuit of fame and fortune. Dating men in the business only produced heart aches, and marrying one brought me to the brink of bankruptcy.

I glanced over at Robbie in the kitchen, leaning on a cabinet, giving out orders over the phone. Just a normal guy with a real job. So cool and confident, and hot—in his faded jeans, boots, tight in-all-the-right-places black t-shirt, and an old ball cap on his head. He's so sexy in uniform, and out of it.

He caught me staring as he finished his call, and his lips twerked. "I'm ready for something stronger. How about you?" He asked, and it took me a moment to realize he meant alcohol, not relationships.

He grabbed an amber bottle and a couple of glasses from a cabinet, and I followed him and his perfect ass in those jeans back to his small couch where he sat and poured the drinks.

"Here. Nothing like Kentucky bourbon to help you sleep. If you're worried about things, that is."

Since I couldn't say I wasn't worried, I took the glass and sat opposite him with barely a cushion length between us. The sip wasn't bad. I took another and relished how quickly my insides warmed up.

I sunk back into the couch, bringing my knees into my chest, and between the warmth of his sweatshirt and the alcohol, I was perfectly cozy. "Mm. I've never had this. I'm more of a beer or wine drinker myself."

"Whoa there," he stopped me as I attempted a third sip in a matter of seconds. "Bourbon is meant to be savored, darling. Take it slow."

"*Darling.* I like that Southern charm and the little twang that comes out in your words now and then."

The corners of his lips barely perked up at that compliment, as he took a sip of his.

"Did I say something wrong?" I asked.

"No. Just...trying to remain calm and cool, and not freak out that a rock star is in my house."

I bristled a bit and nodded toward the albums. "Yes, you're quite the fan with my entire collection over there, but I'm more than that, you know. I'm a real person with a whole life outside of rock and roll."

"Really?"

His arched eyebrow and reply hit a nerve. Unsure myself, who the hell was I outside of singing on a stage or acting in a movie anymore? The only thing I knew, while taking in the profile of this handsome police officer beside me, was how desperately I wanted to find out exactly who he was, especially out of his clothes.

It'd been almost two years since Bruce and I...Ugh, I didn't want to think of him, not while Robbie sat next to me, exuding more sexual energy than Bruce did in all our years during our pathetic marriage.

After another sip of Bourbon, my eyes grew heavy, but I wasn't ready to retire yet. Sitting so close to the lawman, the chemistry between us boiled, heating me up. I wanted to know if it did for him, too.

"Why Robbie, not Rob or Robert?" I asked.

"This is the south and a small town. People start calling you something, it sticks. In school and sports, my parents used to yell *Robbie* and soon the whole town was, too."

"And what does your girlfriend call you?" I fished, eyeing him above the rim of my glass while *savoring* another sip. Considering he lived here alone, I hoped there wasn't one.

He chuckled and scrubbed at his five o'clock shadow. "My ex called me a whole slew of words when we broke up a few years ago, but I won't repeat them for you."

"Hm. Sounds like a story there. Tell me."

"You really want to know?"

"Yep." I repositioned with my legs under me, knees pointing toward him, and my arm across the back of the couch. "Since you're protecting me, I want to know what makes you tick."

His jaw set and he shifted, too, facing me, one knee resting on the cushion. "Okay. Merry and I were high school sweethearts. Her dad, Mac, was the town police chief at the time. She was the youngest of six sisters, but her oldest sister disappeared without a trace."

"Oh no. How awful."

He took a healthy nip of the drink and sighed, as if something haunted him talking about this, but continued. "Mac was a good friend of my Dad's, and good to me and Meadow. He's one of the reasons why I became a cop. I wanted to be like him, plus help him find his daughter. We tried and tried to solve the case, almost obsessed with it, but never could get anywhere."

"Hm. And what about Merry?"

"We broke up when she went off to college, then years later she returned. We reconnected and tried to see if we could make it work as adults, all the while her parents grew more and more distraught. Her mother, especially, could never get over the loss of her daughter."

"Well, how did it end?"

"Mac decided to retire. By then, his wife gave up, convinced the girls to leave town, start over someplace new, where they wouldn't be reminded of their loss. But Mac couldn't leave. So they parted ways, and he stayed, just in case she ever returned."

"So sad. That must have been heartbreaking for them." One of my love languages being affection, it couldn't be helped that I reached over and touched his thigh. Oh, the heat, the hard muscle, his eyes shifting to stare at my hand there...big mistake. A sizzling jolt of energy blasted through me until I removed it. "Why didn't you move away with Merry?"

"I was appointed chief of police, taking over when Mac retired, the youngest officer ever to hold the position. He trained me well, and I jumped in with both feet and took it on, but the job took its toll on our relationship. She, uh, cheated with some stranger who was passing through town. We were pretty much over by then anyway, and I had no intention of ever leaving Kissing Springs."

"Yikes. So...you're over her?"

"Oh yes. It took some time, but I'm good now. Besides...I realized she had one major flaw I couldn't overlook."

"And that was?"

"She wasn't a fan of rock and roll." He said it so seriously at first, then winked and broke out in a laugh. He tossed his hat on the table and ran a hand through his hair, leaving it sexy and unruly. Oh, I liked him.

The more time I spent with him, the more my trust in him grew. He seemed so...good, and I'd never dated a good guy before. Lots of morally gray ones, lots of bad boys, but none like Robbie.

Could he be the one to heal me? To break down my fears about picking the wrong man again, and prove to me how I could land a decent man for once?

"So...you're never leaving Kissing Springs?" I asked, for clarity's sake.

He gazed my direction, sad, as if searching for something in my eyes a long time before he spoke. "No."

He'd never leave...well, I wasn't one for making long-term plans right now, anyway. Taking things one day at a time was more my pace these days, and sitting right here, inches away from a man I'd felt more attracted to than any other in my life, I had nowhere else I'd rather be.

Kissing Springs grew on me, and so did he, looking hotter by the minute.

This was insane...and driving me crazy for him. I sensed our attraction and, at the same time, his hesitation when it came to me. Would he ever dare take things further between us? Let out his inner bad boy for my pleasure only? Cuff me, take me to bed, and use all his dirty words to seduce me?

I was ready to trust, to try again—and desperate for physical touch, but something told me I'd need to make the first move. This man was too good of a guy to let himself go any further down the road with the bad girl.

Lucky for him, I wouldn't let that stop me. According to my critics, I wasn't just a diva, but the baddest girl in modern rock. I'd always been this way, pushing the envelope where I could. With Robbie—when I saw a man I wanted, I made him mine.

CHAPTER 11

BECAUSE...THE NIGHT WITH YOU

PRIMA

"I HAPPEN to know a woman who would be perfect for you." Wow, taking my last sip of bourbon, with my insides warm, I was feeling very empowered.

"Oh, yeah?" His brows shot up.

I set my glass down on the coffee table and faced him. "Yes, and she loves guys who love rock music."

His signature sly smile grew in one corner of his mouth. "Maybe I need to meet this woman."

"I don't know, though. She's just gone through a nasty divorce, and her heart is on the mend. She'd need to be handled with care."

He chewed his cheek. "Hm. Sounds like a big red flag to me."

"No. She's ready. You see, the last guy didn't treat her right. So many things he could have done to keep her and didn't. Really, it had been over for a while." I leaned in closer to him, my hand landing next to his thigh on the cushion.

"Maybe she should give her heart time to heal. Not be so quick to jump into something new." His eyes stared deeply into mine, like a warning. I ignored it.

"But what she wants most is to believe that there could be a decent man out there who knows how to treat a woman right. What I want to know is... Are you that man?"

"Prima—"

"Melody," I said.

"Huh?"

I shifted closer, reducing the space between us. With my knees tucked under me and my arm on the back cushion, I was level with him, able to stare right into his comforting eyes. "My real name is Melody."

His brows stitched together. "Wow, I've never heard that bit of trivia before."

"You wouldn't. The court records changing the name were sealed. It's a long story."

"I told you mine. Come on, spill yours. I mean, if you want."

"I shouldn't have even mentioned it." I side-eyed him. Was I taking this newfound trust I had in him too far?

"You know, the one thing I like about being a cop in a small town is the relationships I've developed with the townsfolk. I swore an oath to protect them. They know me; they trust me. I'm here for you and you can trust me, too."

God, he was solid, and I didn't mean just in body build. The emotional maturity he exuded was years beyond my ex. With every second that ticked by, my feelings for him grew.

After a big sigh, I let out the secret I'd been harboring for ages. "Our mother was a singer by night, raising us by day. We often fell asleep in the dressing room at whatever nightclub Lucy performed late at night. Sara and I called each one a sleepover and built forts in the dressing rooms."

I smiled at happier times, then continued. "Mom always had music on in the house, and the three of us often sang and danced. Sara's voice was way better than mine, more clear and soulful. But by ten, I developed a love for Lucy's old classic rock records and started naturally developing the husky, raspy alto."

I looked away across the room, remembering the time like it had just happened. "One day, Mom brought home an agent she was dating to meet us. We both performed for him. Only Sara was shy. I wasn't and belted out a Janis Joplin number. The dickhead took one look at Sara with her crooked teeth and nose and one look at me, and determined I'd be the one my mother could make the most money off of. Only my name was too sweet. 'Melody hardly sounds like a rock star's name,' he'd said. Mom hired a lawyer the next day to change it."

"Jeez, that's rough. Did you want to change it?"

"No. From that day forward, we weren't allowed to speak it again. It was hardest for Sara. She'd called me Mellie all our lives. Mom spent all her money on me to develop my talent, and none on Sara. It wasn't fair. That's why I've always tried to take care of her, always having Sara work for me through the years."

I shook my head. I didn't know where either of us would be if none of the past had happened. It was what it was, and no sense wishing it were any different. I just knew, if I was ever a mother like Sara, I'd be better for my kid, or I'd die trying.

"I like Melody and Mellie for you. It fits." He cocked his head and locked his eyes with mine. "But Prima is unique. Where did that come from, if you don't mind me asking?"

"Well, you'll get a laugh out of this. From the Premiere Pasta box from the spaghetti we ate that night after Mom's boyfriend left. She said if I was going to be the best, I'd need the best name."

I chuckled and rolled my eyes. "Oh God, hearing myself tell you all of this, I feel as though my life has been one big joke."

"No, it hasn't. Maybe with your mother it wasn't the best beginning, but your music struck a chord with people all these years or else you wouldn't be where you are today—a highly regarded woman in rock. Own that shit."

My eyes flashed to him. "God, I needed to hear that. You really are one good man, aren't you, chief?"

He snickered and looked away, as if brushing off the compliment I just gave. This humble man, so strong and steadfast—I wasn't sure how much longer I could go without touching him. The desire for his arms around me and his body rocking with mine peaked.

"Seriously, though, you are," I whispered. Turned out, I couldn't wait a second longer. I moved and straddled his lap, the look on his face a mixture of shock, fear and lust.

Cupping his cheeks, I purred. "I see you, Robbie. You're so caring, so strong for everyone. You're my protector, and I like it."

My lips were about to re-engage with his, dying to feel the fullness of them again after our kiss in the bar. An inch away, with my heart beating wildly in my chest—he stopped me with one hand on my arm.

"Whoa there, darling. I have a rule. Never get personally attached to a case. I've already taken things too far having you here," he said.

Not one to give up until I got what I wanted, I wasn't deterred. He didn't exactly throw me off his lap either. I removed the glass from his hand and set it on the table next to the couch. "I'm not a case. I'm flesh and blood and curves and a woman who desires you."

"And a diva who's used to getting what she wants?" He smirked.

"You catch on quick." My lips brushed along the whiskers of his jaw until I hit his soft earlobe. A growl emitted from his chest and I smiled while sucking in and teasing his lobe with my tongue because the good cop couldn't hide how hard he was. I shifted against him, seeking my own relief against the hardness in his jeans.

His hands slowly roamed up my thighs. "Mm. Mellie, we shouldn't start what we can't finish."

My insides flipped. "You using my real name makes me want you even more," I spoke on his skin, my lips finally landing on his and oh, they were good. So full, so soft. He kissed back tenderly. My heart skipped several beats lingering here with him.

"We shouldn't... My rule..." I drowned the agony in his voice with another kiss.

I pulled apart just enough to connect with his eyes. "Even a good man like you should know...rules were made to be broken. Break one with me, *darling*." I copied his southern drawl on the last word while grinding on his lap. His hands landed on my hips, guiding my movements.

"Why me? You could have your pick of any man."

"Because, this night, with you protecting me, turned me on."

"Goddamn, you're a seductress, baby. What are you doing to me?"

"I'm starting a fire. Don't fight it. You know you want me, Robbie."

"Fuck. I do. But my brain is telling me to snuff it out before it turns into a wildfire."

"What does your heart say?"

The curved corner of his mouth spoke volumes. "It's reminding me that wild things can't be contained, but to take the ride and hold on for as long as I can."

His arms drew me in, and his tongue split my lips. He deepened our kisses, then this strong man lifted us both off the couch, his hands cupping my ass. With my legs wrapped around him, I clung to his neck, continuing to nip and suck there on his skin. He smelled of leather and musk and trust and all the things I expected a man like him to exude.

At his bed, he laid me down so carefully, like he didn't want me to break—even here playing the protector, watching out for me. While other men would have torn my clothes off by now, he was a slow burn, a neat glass of bourbon, something to be savored with every sip...every touch.

I'd never been so turned on in all my life. My panties were soaked; my clit died for his touch. He knelt between my legs, and his lips brushed down my neck as he moved lower. With elbows on either side of me, his hands lifted the KSPD sweatshirt and my tank top with it, exposing the tattoo on my right rib.

"There it is," he gazed. "I always wondered in the photo of you on your last album cover if the tattoo was real or not."

"Considering it hurt like hell having it done...very real."

"And very appropriate." He licked and sucked every letter across the word *Temptress,* inked permanently on my skin.

I'd gotten the tattoo in defiance of Bruce, who hated the idea of my body having any markings at all, and worried it made me less likely to gain roles in movies. But at that point in our marriage, I'd had enough of his control, and it was the beginning of the end.

I recall meeting with the tattoo artist going over design ideas. I wanted nothing too flashy or over the top. Just a statement. When I saw the word Temptress in gorgeous lettering, I knew it was the one.

I'd gotten the tattoo for me, not him. And now, Robbie was the first man to touch it.

CHAPTER 12

LOVE SHACKING UP

ROBBIE

*TEMPTRESS...*I had no doubt Prima *was* one, both on stage and under the sheets.

Being honest with myself, since the moment she waltzed into my town, my cock ached for her, bulging against my zipper, begging to give this wild baby a ride and test her limits. My mouth wouldn't stop kissing every inch of tanned, toned skin showing. In seconds, I could have her naked.

Instead, with *everything* I could muster—damn, this was a true test of my willpower—I stopped. I shifted up onto my knees, still lodged between her legs, and gazed into eyes so green they could be authentic gems.

"You're thinking too hard about this," she said, and cocked her head and chuckled. She lifted and removed my sweatshirt and her tank top, tossing them together into a jumbled mess onto the floor.

Mess...that would be a fine word for a tryst with this woman, and exactly why we shouldn't.

I wasn't an idiot, though; I fully eye-fucked her breasts in a black satin bra with my tongue hanging out, licking my bottom lip. One twist of the strap would be all it would take, and I'd toss that on the floor, too. But I didn't.

I shook my head, and hated the cop in me, the adult in me, preventing every fantasy from playing out in my bed with her. "Someone has to think before we take things too far."

"My thoughts are *perfectly* clear. I want you," she said, in almost a bratty tone. I had a mind to toss her over my knee and deal out my own punishment for her tempting me to break my rule. "And I know you want me, too."

"What makes you so sure?" I smirked.

"For obvious reasons." Her eyes fell with a nod to my crotch. Yep, my thick buddy was a dead giveaway, about to bust down the doors I kept slamming shut on him. "And because you're still on your knees in front of me."

I was—as if the sheets were made of super glue.

Her hands caressed down her body, landing at the button of her jeans. She plucked it open. I swallowed hard.

She was a dangerous dare and a tantalizing truth in one beautiful babe, waiting on my mattress for me—no—

seducing me in my own bed.

"I'm usually the one in control," I said.

"Not tonight," she purred.

I liked her way of thinking. Fifty million decisions I had to make daily as the Police Chief, and tonight the only decision I had was a simple fuck yes or hell no. But it wasn't that easy.

The zipper of her jeans was the accompaniment to my heart beating fast, creating a crazy rhythm in my ears. As she shimmied them past her hips, past her ass, the apex of her thighs appeared in a matching black satin pair of panties. The scent of her called to me like a goddamn siren.

"Be a sweetie and remove my booties and jeans." She lifted one long leg in the air, almost landing on my chest.

"Mellie..." I strained through gritted teeth.

"Pretty please," she mewed, batting her lashes up at me, and twirling a lock of her hair through her fingers.

I chuckled and shook my head. "Does that work with every man?"

"Only you."

Fuck me. I did as she asked, first the left, then the right, and her jeans ended up in the same pile on the floor.

My God. The rock star diva, my temptress, splayed out before me. I needed a moment to revere the goddess she was with a wink and a nod to my younger self, the guy who probably jerked off to an album cover of hers a time or two.

I memorized every inch of her body, every curve. There was no getting away from her now. Even if I could tear myself away to sleep on the couch, I'd be up all night long climbing the walls, dying to know what it's like to be inside of her.

She reached for me, balling the hem of my shirt in her fists, and pulled me on top of her. I succumbed to her strength, and hovered above on my elbows, so close, her leg raised and crossed over my buttocks.

Rock hard, my cock a dead giveaway, she discovered my truth, moving beneath me, gyrating her hips against me.

"I just need to feel desired by a man again. Help me with that, chief," she whispered.

"I do desire you, but..." Fuck, I wanted her. Both her ankles crossed at my back now, her center rocked against my shaft. With her breath hitching, her half lidded orbs, the woman could make me come in my pants any second.

"What are you afraid of? Little old me?" She teased. Her arms circled around my neck, and she pulled herself closer, sucking in my bottom lip and moaning. My resolve wilted away.

When my lip popped out of her mouth, I took her arms and pinned them down above her head. My body flattened on top of hers, and I nuzzled her neck, nipping and sucking her skin. Her flowery scent surrounded me.

"Yes, Robbie," she moaned my name in a voice so sweet and breathy, driving me insane.

"If I let myself go with you, I'll want more than just tonight," I warned.

"From what I can tell, the size of you, I'll want more too," she chuckled breathlessly.

"Things could get complicated." I plowed against her and growled. My cock had had enough, ready to tear the fabric between us.

"Ooh, I'm counting on it. Let's fuck and see where this goes."

"Holy hell, you *are* a temptress," I roared, giving in. I dropped to my side and rolled onto my back. How eager I was, after she'd seduced me this far, to see what else she'd do to me. "Take control, darling."

"With pleasure." A smile split her face and my fly was the first thing she attacked, undoing it with ease. I lifted, and she tugged my jeans down, not bothering to remove my boots and the rest. She focused on one thing—my thick cock—and he wasn't complaining.

Like unwrapping a package, she peeled just enough of my Calvin's back to show my glorious tip, glistening like a boast with pre-cum. I pulled a pillow over to prop up my head, because I wasn't missing a minute of this.

As she lowered her mouth on me, she peered up with a satisfied smile. Then her tongue, ungh, what she could do with it, twirling around me. Her fingertips tugged at my boxers, and finally, my entire shaft was free, twitching for her attention.

"God, you're beautiful," she admired me, then wrapped her lips around my cock, sucking down the pole.

I gathered her hair in my fist and guided her movements. My other hand caressed her cheek, but she felt so damn good deep throating me, I had to move. I pulsed my hips, hitting the back of her throat, and she took every inch.

"Good girl," I groaned and praised. She hummed and added a fist, stroking me, her pace quickening, her head bobbing. It's all too much, too fast, too heated from the start. "Jeez, Mellie, you have me coming undone already."

Electric currents shot down my body, curling my toes, and she moaned as the first drops of cum hit her throat. She sucked me deeper and deeper, milking me dry, and swallowed every ounce. I closed my eyes and was gone, high above the earth in some stratosphere where it's perfectly natural for a regular guy like me to get sucked off by a rock queen.

When I heard a slick pop, my cock released from her mouth. I lazily opened my eyes, watching her tuck me back into my boxers and giving it a pet.

"Good boy," she grinned, looking almost as satisfied as I was right now.

"Come here." I pulled her over and shifted onto my side, spooning with her back to me. Her head rested on my right arm; with my other, I danced fingertips down her curves, over her shoulder, and played with her magenta curls. "You're fucking sexy as hell, but I think you know that."

"I'd never grow tired of hearing you say it, in case you were wondering, for future information."

"Yeah, something tells me you like your ego stroked."

"Among other things," she purred, and took control again, pushing my hand down her stomach to her panties. I wasted no time sliding under the satin, letting my middle finger part her slick seam.

"Fucking wet for me, baby." I growled in her ear, tracing her lobe with my tongue.

When I parted her folds, I caressed her clit, and tested various depths of pressure. Judging by her moans and squirms, I found the one that hit perfectly.

"Right there, chief. Don't stop," she begged.

Her leg lifted on me, shaking, and widening my access. On one elbow, I rose and watched her face, in all its contortions, during each stage of her ecstasy. So soon, my cock came alive again, knocking on her back door.

"Mm. I'm close. Please, can I feel you inside of me?" She asked, bucking her sweet ass against me.

"Yes, but let's get some things squared away. Are you on the pill?"

"Of course. Even though it's been a few years for me since my ex," she said.

"A couple of years for me, too." Way too fucking long. "Does that mean we can—"

"Slide it in. Now." She ordered.

"I'll let you have control tonight, but next time it's my turn." I smirked at my demanding babe, and stood to remove my boots and clothes. She squirmed out of her bra and panties, giving me full view of her.

"You're fucking beautiful, Mellie." I didn't waste another minute, freed of the burden of having to retrieve a condom.

With her leg straight in the air, I repositioned behind her, holding onto it for leverage. Slowly from behind, I entered her, inch by tight inch, savoring the feel of her wet walls engulfing me in her heat.

"So good, baby. Play with yourself until you come on my cock." I kissed her thigh, pulling back out, then plunged back into her.

"Yes," she begged. "More like that." This woman knew exactly what she wanted, and I was the pleaser, more than happy to give it.

Like any great rock anthem, I started slowly, in and out, building up the desire as if it wasn't there already between us. Through a chorus of her moans, I quickened the pace, driving her wild. I held on tight, gritting my teeth, holding myself back, making sure she came first.

With a face like an angel in the throes of ecstasy, my name sung from her lips as a repeated refrain, one I begged to hear over and over. From the start, we'd connected and now proved we could make the perfect music together in bed. She was the songstress, and I was the protector, from opposite worlds, yet somehow we made sense.

She chased me to get here, seduced me with her wily ways. The temptress won me over. Now I was chasing her, driving her to the edge, deepening my charge. I growled and speared into her, and her body shattered under me, coming apart.

"Yes, Robbie. Oh, yeah," she screamed. The big finish to our song arrived. I came undone, coming hard with a roar.

At first, I had resisted her, but her temptations were too strong. Now that I knew how intense it was to be inside of her, one time would never be enough. This first was just the beginning.

I slowly released her leg and hovered over her. Through labored breathing, we kissed, soft and sweet. "I'm glad you talked me into this." Our foreheads met and we laughed together.

"Maybe next time I won't have to work so hard to convince you."

I kissed her nose. "Next time, *I'll* be in control. Be prepared."

"I like the sound of that."

So did I. I wanted more, but there was the familiar pull of the badge, as I left her to get a cloth to clean us up.

My old worries crept in about being too involved with someone, too close to a case. When emotions were at play, it was hard to remain objective and think on your feet in difficult—sometimes life-threatening—situations.

Too late now. As I held her in my arms all night, I knew I was getting in with her deep, blurring the lines between protector and lover.

CHAPTER 13

WE'RE COMING AROUND

ROBBIE

SETTING aside my loyalties to the badge for once, the man in me had to admit—damn, it was fucking good to break my dry spell. Prima sleeping in my arms all night had me believing she had a good time. Good enough for a second round?

I ground some dark roast coffee beans in the kitchen, smiling over the memories of a night with her I'd never forget. She had her fun. Now I'd love nothing more than to have mine, taking her any way I pleased.

I could, this morning, charge right into my room and bury my cock between her legs again. But she slept so soundly, rolling over back to sleep when I left the bed.

Besides, after last night's fiasco at the bar, I needed to check in at work. She had things to do, too. We both had lives, and just because we spent a night together didn't mean we were tethered down.

My cock twitched, clearly not on board with my decision.

I turned on the coffee pot and waited for the brewing to begin, planning to deliver a cup to her bedside. Next thing I knew, she slid into the kitchen and stood beside me, wearing nothing but my KSPD sweatshirt. Damn, if she was naked underneath, I might let her keep it.

"Mornin' darling. How do you take yours?"

"Warm for my throat, and strong, with a side of anything you have for a headache," she chuckled, her fingertips massaging the back of her head.

"I've got the perfect remedy." I moved behind her, shifted her locks to the side, and massaged her shoulders to release her trigger points. "And another reason to touch you."

Her little moan satisfied me. "You don't need a special reason. Touch me anytime."

She shouldn't have said that, now my brain went hard at work thinking of when, where, how.

"Oh, that feels nice. I haven't had a good massage since I've been back in Kissing Springs."

"My fingers are at your service. I'll check my schedule and see how soon I'm free for that." I kissed the back of her neck and my cock jutted out from my gray sweats.

Another minute of kneading and touching her skin and my dick would rage for some massaging of his own.

The coffee maker chimed, saving me from taking her right here. "Better?" I asked.

"Mm-hmm. Now I know the wide range of talents you have with your fingers."

"I've only just begun to show you my talents." I snickered and filled our mugs. We both leaned against the counter while taking the first sips of the day.

This was nice. I might like to have more of these mornings with her while she was in town. And after? Her life was in California, mine here. None of this made sense right now, so there's no point driving myself crazy.

She seemed more free spirited than me. I was the over thinker. While she's probably looking forward to our next fuck, and I was, too, my head swam with thoughts about after. I wished I could be more like her and take things as they come.

"By the way, I never did thank you," she said, breaking into my thoughts.

"For what? Last night? I should be the one thanking you." I smoldered my grin her way.

Her laughter filled the kitchen, a sound I could get accustomed to after living alone far too long. "You're most welcome. But seriously, this summer, when I needed help after escaping from my mother's place, you hardly knew me. Yet you sprung into action when Sara and Charles called, pulling strings and working your cop magic. Somehow, within an hour, that police friend of yours, Officer Trevor, came to the rescue picking me up and delivering me to Mick's private airplane so I could fly back here to be with Sara."

"No thanks necessary. When Charles told me you were in trouble, I made some calls and cashed in a few favors."

"But you didn't have to, Robbie. You hardly knew me then."

"I knew enough. Besides, when someone is in trouble, I can't ignore it. If there's something I can do to help, I'll do it. It's in my nature. Why do you think I became a police officer?"

"You're a good man. Maybe too good for me." Her stare my way above her coffee mug held a strain of vulnerability I'd bet she rarely showed to the outside world.

"I would have felt a lot better if you'd have let Trevor arrest your mother that night, too."

"I know. He's asked me a few times if I've changed my mind about that."

"Really? You're, uh, still in touch with him?" Not only did a hint of jealousy strike me, which I ignored, but it was curious. Like a flipped switch, my radar was up, back into police mode.

"He texts me now and then to see how I'm doing."

Shit. Could Trevor be the stalker? Was he here somewhere in Kissing Springs? I wasn't that good of a friend with him, only an acquaintance from the police academy, but I knew he had family here and he'd stopped in a few times at my station over the years when he visited.

It wouldn't be too inconceivable that he could travel back to town, take photos of Prima, and easily get way too close to her. But why didn't she put him on the list of people she knew as we were looking into the stalking case?

One by one, my officers interviewed and eliminated her entourage, her hairdresser, and other industry professionals —none of them were in town to take photos of Prima at the store, or Prima and I at the pie shop.

We were chasing up the whereabouts of her ex, a few old boyfriends, and her band members. But it might have been nice to know about Trevor still being in contact with her.

"Interesting," I said.

"What's that mean?" She eyed me.

"Nothing. Just didn't realize you were still in touch with him."

"Hm. A little jealous? He's a fan, an acquaintance, nothing more."

I set my mug down, took hers, and set it down, too. Then I brought her into my arms, linking my fingers behind her back. "No, I'm not jealous. You know why?"

"Because you're here and he's there?"

"Yeah. Look who has you in his arms this morning, beautiful." I pressed a kiss on her forehead. "Besides, I'm a fan of Prima onstage, but I'm getting to be an even bigger fan of Melody with every second I spend with her."

"Oh, my God. If you think I go for that sappy stuff...you're right. In fact, you had me the second I walked in here and you greeted me with *Mornin', darling.*" She tried to imitate my voice, unsuccessfully, making me crack up.

"You're so fucking irresistible." I leaned down for a kiss, slipping my tongue in with hers. She put up no resistance and threaded her fingers into my hair, pulling me in, deepening our connection. All the blood drained from my brain and flooded into my cock and screw it, the rest of the world could wait.

I needed more of her. Now.

My hand slid under the sweatshirt, gliding up the soft skin of her thigh, and just like I thought—she was naked underneath.

"Yes, Robbie."

"Yes, what?"

"Yes, you can fuck me right here, right now." She read my mind, and purred with sexual confidence, lighting me up.

I pushed the sweatshirt up and over her head, tossing it on the counter. Her breasts bared to me with pert nipples readied for my touch. My mouth sucked them in, one at a time, savoring each with a swirl of my tongue, hardening them to pebbles.

The slick entry of two of my fingers into her wet center was made even easier as her leg rode up my thigh. Her face contorted with her moan, as her head fell back over my arm, letting her hair fall freely. In the middle of the kitchen, standing, supporting us, I had her squirming in my arms, and I was ready to give this rock star a ride.

She lifted her head, eyeing me through half-lidded domes. This beauty who stole my breath every time with her eyes so clear and green, knew what she wanted. Her hand drifted down and plucked my cock from my sweats and stroked it, spreading the pre-cum until my head glistened.

"Hold on tight, baby." Not wasting another second, I lifted her up onto me, her legs hooking behind me. I held her ass in place, and somehow my cock found its way and slid into her like he knew which way was home. One long growl vibrated through my chest, welcoming the feel of her tight walls, cradling me, possessing me again.

Soon we were skin to skin, breathing hard, with every motion in sync. Her head buried into my neck, holding onto me, and her silky hair tickled my shoulder, but I wouldn't let up until we were both satisfied.

"You're so strong. My protector." Her praise served me well, powering me through.

If the kitchen was the stage, then I rocked it right now, taking everything in me to keep us standing and fucking. But I couldn't last much longer.

"I like this with you, Mellie," I said through clenched teeth.

"Me, too," came her breathy reply. "And I want more of this while I'm here."

That was everything I needed to know. More. Her. Us. Even if only for a short time. And before I dwelled on that too much, I thrust one final time, holding her in place on me. I groaned through my release, filling her up, until my legs almost gave out.

On the counter, I set her ass there and buried my head between her sweet breasts, trying to calm down from it all. I liked her sexy ways, our banter, every second with her.

"I'll take more of this, too." I kissed her breast. "And this." I leaned down and kissed the mound at the apex of her thighs. "And definitely a million more kisses from a rock star." Our lips collided, hot and hungry, until they had their fill.

As I was about to carry her to the shower so she could clean up, her face fell. I hooked her chin with my finger and pulled it up, and worry clouded her eyes. "Uh-oh. What'd I say to cause that face?"

She sighed, shrugging it off. "It's just a conversation I always find myself having when I start dating someone. We can't tell anyone about us."

My head jerked back. "Okay. Why not?"

"Because you'd be hounded by the fame seekers, the cameras, the media. Your life would turn upside down, you'd be offered money for exclusive interviews, and for a blip in time you'd even have some star status, all because you'd be seen with me."

How many men had she had to have this conversation with? I smoothed her hair back off her face and stopped that thought right now. "We're just coming around to the good stuff, getting to know each other, so let me clue you in. First of all, I couldn't care less about all the fame and attention. That's your world and I'm happy for you, but my face splattered across social media isn't for me."

"And the second?"

"It's not like I'm walking out the door and broadcasting the news of how I slept with you. Hell, rumors spread fast in a small town, and the old biddies could give Hollywood news a run for their money." I chuckled, but it was true. "If any of the gossiping women in town saw me walking hand in hand or kissing you, they'd start a betting pool for our wedding date."

"Very funny, but I'd bet Hollywood is more ruthless than the old ladies at Sunday church. If we could just agree to keep us a secret, it would make things a lot easier."

"Secret lovers?" I arched a brow.

"Exactly."

"You mean because you're only here for a short time, so why complicate things?"

"Yes. I'm so glad you understand." Her arms wrapped around me while I weighed this...this...situation.

Keeping things a secret would make my life easier without the speculation of everyone in the township. I didn't like people in my business, whispering behind my back.

Secrecy would be a reminder that whatever the situation-ship we were in had an expiration date when she left Kissing Springs. That could make it easier on me when she leaves.

It could help me compartmentalize my roles. Robbie, the Chief, serving and protecting, versus Robbie under the sheets serving up good loving. Hey, it was sex, and considering I hadn't had much in the past few years, this would be an improvement.

"Well, if that's what you want," I shrugged.

"Yes. I always get what I want." She winked.

"Don't I know it. Now come on, time for a shower." I carried her off in my arms to the bathroom, where I started up the water for her.

"Nice. Be careful, chief. I could get used to this," she said, and I watched her luscious body disappear behind the shower curtain.

So could I. And that was the problem.

CHAPTER 14

DRAGGING MY HEART ALLOVER

PRIMA

WHY DID I agree to attend this fall bonfire rally for the homecoming game of the local high school football team? I suddenly felt like I was in an episode of Home Sweet Home.

Families were everywhere, kids running around, parents, grandparents, multiple generations, all hung out in the parking lot at the school, gathered around a raging fire in the middle. A few firemen were around, tending to the flames to ensure everyone was safe.

The band played the school's song over and over. The cute cheerleaders kept the crowd going with their spirit, shaking their pom-poms all about. And the guys on the team in their jerseys riled everyone up.

I accompanied Sara and Charles and the twins there, and of course Dillon and Meadow met up with us there. While Kissing Springs kind of grew on me, I felt very much the odd one out with no one of my own and no tie to the community.

I had to admit, though, I fancied all their fun. Never having a normal childhood myself, I wondered what life might have been like with a mother and a father, a hometown, and me in a cheerleading uniform.

Sara and I never knew our dad. Lucy never could recall which man she'd slept with who unwittingly donated his sperm to give us life. We used to dream he was a prince, or a famous star, or the president. Never once did we dream of an ordinary man, working nine-to-five, with a family living paycheck to paycheck in a tiny town barely a dot on a map.

By the time we were of high school age, my career had taken off. Between concerts and a small recurring role on a family television show, Sara and I were taught by tutors. So all of this tonight was a bit much to take in.

"Isn't this great?" Sara beamed, fitting right into all of this. I nodded. Years down the road, her children might be a football captain or homecoming queen here, and she'd be the best mom ever.

What about me? I hugged my sides. How much longer would I be able to rock the stage? In all of Lucy's preaching to Sara and me about what life was like as a celebrity, I didn't recall a single conversation about life after stardom, or life without it. But surely, at some point, my star would burn out and what then?

Eventually, I wandered over to the concession stand, seeking hot chocolate or coffee, something to take the chill off this night, although I could use something stronger. Only when I got in line, I spotted the one man who was my tether to this community. I just couldn't share that fact with anyone.

Robbie stood tall and gallant in his blue uniform, talking with a fireman. Suddenly, a couple of kids ran up to them. The boy jumped into the arms of the fireman, the girl into Robbie's, and I choked. Seeing him interacting with kids, I realized I had never once thought of him as a potential father until now.

Then a woman came up to them, hugged both men, and settled next to the fireman. As they talked, Robbie's mannerisms, the way he smiled and bounced the girl in his arms, and a certain look in his eyes tore me up.

Did he want a family? Was I being selfish keeping Robbie on the line for my own amusement when he could be out finding Mrs. Right-at-home-in-a-small-town?

Over the past week, we'd been successfully keeping our situation under wraps. If we ran into each other in town or at the studios, we'd say hi, and keep the flirting to a minimum. No one was any wiser, so I thought.

It was our nights where things got more eventful. Behind closed doors, we were free to explore. In the dark, I'd come knocking, and he'd let me into his cottage, into his bed, into the safety of his arms. I'd finally found a way to a good night's sleep through sex and snuggles with him, then afterwards I slept like a baby until he brought me coffee in bed each morning.

It worked for me. What about him?

"Ma'am? What would you like?" The kid behind the counter caught my attention. I hadn't realized the line moved and now it was my turn to order.

"Pumpkin spiced hot cocoa, please."

"Holy shit. You're that rock star," the pimple-faced teen exclaimed.

"Make that two, Connor, and I'll pay." Robbie's deep twang called out as he stepped beside me and tossed a few bills on the counter.

The guy snapped to attention. "Yes, sir."

"How is our resident celebrity doing tonight? Enjoying the bonfire?" Robbie asked professionally, not looking at me, his face straight ahead.

"Oh, I think the real celebrities are the football team," I chuckled.

Connor returned with the styrofoam cups, then with a hand shaking held out a napkin and a ball-point pen. "Um. Ma'am," his voice cracked. I knew what was coming. "Can I get your autograph? My brother, Andrew, is a Knight, and I've been begging him to introduce me to you. I've been teaching myself guitar and writing some songs. I think your work is awesome."

"Tell you what," I said as I signed the napkin. "Why don't you come down to the studios next week with your guitar? I'll give you a tour and sign the back of that, too."

"What? Seriously? Oh, you just made my night." Connor flashed a grin full of braces at me.

As we walked away, Robbie said under his breath, "That was nice. And you couldn't have found a more needy kid to give a boost like that. I know Andrew and his brothers struggle without a father, and they're good kids. You have no idea how much I want to pull you in for a hug right now."

"That's it? Just a chaste little hug?"

"You know better." His coy smile appeared, breaking from the professional stance he had a minute ago.

It turned out his appreciation and his heat next to me warmed more than the cocoa did. I stood taller, and people left and right waved hello to Robbie as we walked. "Look at you, the handsome chief. Seems like *you're* the star getting the most attention around here."

"There's only one woman I want giving a certain part of me attention tonight."

"And which part is that?" My insides fluttered, knowing how the night would end in his bed.

"You know damn well it's the hardest part," he smirked. I did, and besides his arms around me, his cock inside of me was the one thing I craved all the time.

Up ahead, I eyed Meadow, Dillon, and the couple Robbie had been talking to before. We were headed straight for them, bringing my time alone with him to a close for now, and I hated it. While they all held hands as couples, I had to keep a safe distance from Robbie.

I couldn't claim him as my man, as the person satisfying my needs every night. I denied myself the pleasure of knowing the simple joys in public, like his hand on my lower back as we walked, or a peck on the cheek as we talked. Little did I know I'd want those things, and I had no one to blame but myself in this situation.

As we arrived at the group, he introduced me. "Prima, this is Tracy and her husband Kipp, longtime friends of mine. Of course, you know Meadow and Dillon."

"Yes. Hi everyone."

"Sorry to run, but Meadow's not feeling good. I should get her home," Dillon said.

"I'm okay, really. I just tried to do too much today," Meadow disagreed. Her baby bump was showing, and admittedly, she was cute as could be in a short flannel plaid dress in fall colors of orange, yellow, and green, over leggings and little boots.

"You've been doing too much with all this wedding planning and your job. I've told you over and over, there's only three things we need the day we marry: You, me, and the guy who says I may now kiss my bride." Aw, Dillon was adorable. I peered up at Robbie and even he didn't have the usual grimace on his face he gets when around either of the Montgomery brothers.

"I agree with Dillon. You made your appearance as mayor. Now get home and rest and take care of my niece or nephew in there. And that's an order." Robbie leaned down and kissed his sister's forehead. Watching him be so protective of his sister like that...oof he was dragging my heart all over the place.

"Fine. We'll catch you all soon," she grumbled, and walked off with Dillon's arm around her.

"Robbie, can I talk to you for a minute?" Kipp thumbed to the side, and the two of them left me alone with Tracy.

She shocked me with a hug like we were instant BFFs. "Oh, look at you. Gorgeous. Welcome to our town. I feel like I know you since I've adopted your sister into our Park Posse."

"The park—what?"

"My little group of moms. We've got each other's backs as we deal daily with life, kids, and husbands," she laughed.

I'd heard plenty about Tracy from Sara, and honestly was a little jealous of their friendship. My sister blossomed here without me, among her new friends and her mom-life.

"I don't know how you all do it day in and day out, juggling kids and everything. And my sister is about to have four children running around her? I'm relieved to hear Sara will have a good support system with other moms." And I meant that sincerely. I wouldn't be much help.

"Here, have a nip of this." She winked, took out a flask, and discreetly poured a little of its contents into my cocoa. She whispered, "A little bourbon here and there, honey. That's one of our secrets."

"Thanks." I sipped and glanced over at Robbie, but he was too intensely involved in a conversation with his buddy to notice.

"So, how long have you had the hots for our chief of police?"

Tracy's question made me almost spit out my drink. I swallowed hard. "Oh, um..."

"Relax, I doubt anyone else noticed but me. I've known Kipp and Robbie as long as I can remember, so I've picked up on a few things here and there. He's got it bad for you. I sense the vibe, and just now seeing you two together, yep, I'm convinced."

Out of the corner of my eye, I saw Robbie and Kipp heading back to us.

"Oh, but really—"

"Deny it if you want, but I know something's going on. I'm happy for you if it is. Robbie is the man *every* woman in town wishes were theirs. I can keep a secret if you need someone to talk to."

Our conversation ended there, when the guys returned, but my deep thoughts on the subject only multiplied.

"Prima, can I give you a ride home?" Robbie asked innocently. "The bonfire is winding down, and my officers can take it from here."

"Sure. It was nice to meet you, Kipp, Tracy." I waved and escaped from them under her all-knowing stare.

Once in the car, I was able to relax.

"You're quiet," Robbie observed, actually driving us to his place instead of taking me home.

"Just stuff weighing me down."

"Let me guess. Tracy thinks there's something going on between us."

"How'd you know?"

"Because Kipp took me to the side and gave me the same rundown," he chuckled. "When you have friends for life, they tend to get all in your business."

"I wouldn't know. Other than Sara, I haven't really had many friends."

"You have me."

He reached over, and finally, in the dark of his vehicle, held my hand. The warmth radiating from it throughout my body had become so familiar, no longer was I certain I could live without it. Or keep it hidden away from the world.

Chapter 15

Uninvited Guest

Prima

"Are you sure Meadow will be fine, that I'm crashing her wedding shower?" I asked for a third time as we parked at the Kissing Springs Playground.

Sara glared at me from the driver's seat of her van. Grace and Hope, Charles' twin daughters, were in back in their car seats.

"Stop worrying. I texted her, and she was fine. This isn't a traditional shower, anyway, since it's a friends and family type of thing. This will be great today. Look, girls, there's your dad." She pointed at Charles, who'd arrived earlier to help Dillon set things up. Squeals came in reply.

"Look! A horse ride," Grace said and pointed to the horses pulling a flatbed with bales of straw for seats.

"They have balloons, Mommy," Hope said. My head snapped to Sara's. It was the first time I heard Hope call my sister that.

Sara shot me a look. "Yes, this is going to be a perfect fall day. Let's go, girls."

We all got out and walked toward the party. I held Grace's hand, while Sara held Hope's. The two littles were so much like us, it wasn't even funny.

Yellow-haired Grace and I were obviously the wild ones. She loved when I played my rock music loud and sang, joining me dancing around Charles' home on the few nights here and there where I babysat for them.

Of course, that was our little secret. I could already tell Sara and Charles would have their hands full with her as she got older.

Sara and Hope were more reserved. Strawberry-blonde Hope with her collections of tiny baby dolls and coloring books, and her love of getting on a barstool and cooking right next to my sister for almost every meal.

Sara wasn't much of a cook, but had taken to working through an entire Betty Crocker's Cookbook, one recipe at a time, to learn. Bless Charles for smiling through burnt roasts and undercooked casseroles.

As we entered the park, how Meadow pulled this off was beyond me. She'd designed a pumpkin patch wedding shower party so kids and families and friends could all take part.

I wasn't thrilled with the thought of it at first, but now I saw there was a little something for everyone: face-painting, hayrides, pumpkin bowling, stacks of hay bales to climb, hide, and tunnel through, and a bounce-house for the kids.

There were plenty of food and drink stations set up, including a barbecue that smelled exactly how I'd picture meat cooked over a spit in the south to be, although the scent of it competed with kettle corn.

For the adults, there were games of chance, like a rubber duck race in a galvanized tub, a corn hole tournament, and a contest for the best carved pumpkin. It was a toss-up whether I'd indulge in a caramel apple or popcorn.

Sara hooked my elbow with her left hand, her new diamond ring blinding me when the sun hit it right. "Run along, Grace and Hope. Have fun!"

They skipped ahead, hand in hand, in their matching leggings and sweaters and little booties, the most fashionable six-year-olds on the planet. I knew Sara had carte blanche from Charles to buy anything for them, and it seemed dressing them up in adorable clothes was her thing.

Then again, Sara and I were also similarly dressed to enjoy the crisp breeze of this fall day.

She lowered her voice to me. "Charles and I talked about it, and decided if the girls wanted to call me mother, they could. Hope has taken right to it. Grace may take some time. He also asked if I wanted to adopt them."

I halted my steps. "Really? I mean yeah. Yeah, that's great."

My twin took to being a mother so naturally, it shouldn't have been a surprise. A part of me was sad, though; Sara had been mine all my life, my twin, and now I had to share her with a husband and four kids.

We'd done almost everything together for years, but she was branching off in new directions. Without me.

It took a little getting used to. Then again, seeing Robbie waving at me from across the way, maybe I had my own path separate from hers, too. Time would tell.

"I told him I'd wait until after we were married, and take some time to think about the adoption," Sara said.

"And *when* are these nuptials taking place?" I hoped she'd tell me quickly as Charles was headed our way.

"Actually, I wanted to talk to you about that. Charles would like to take the whole family somewhere like the Caribbean for Christmas and have an intimate destination wedding." She smiled so widely, I thought her face would split in two.

"But I didn't know if your schedule would allow it. Dillon told me Mick would like to set up a few dates for you to tour in Japan this winter, to test out the new album with more live audiences. He says he loves the tracks Mutt has been sending daily. That's such great news, Prim."

Of course, with any successful album, there'd be a press tour in the major markets, and then a concert tour, so I knew what to expect. But so soon?

So focused was I on making incredible music once again, that I'd forced the rest of the business out of mind. If there's to be a tour, the machine would need to get rolling. From stage concept to costumes, lighting to pyrotechnics, a lot of moving pieces would need decided upon and organized.

Was I ready for a big tour schedule again, to face the grueling grind, city to city?

To leave Kissing Springs?

Robbie seemed to fall into step with Charles, both strapping men heading toward us, and my breath caught. They were dashing, but, once again, the hot cop looked sexy no matter what he was wearing.

This time he appeared the epitome of a small town guy, right at home in a black and red flannel shirt with sleeves folded up his forearms, dark jeans and hiking boots.

Home...Every night together at his place, we connected, and reached a place deeper than I'd felt with a man in quite some time. This morning was even better, laughing with him as we failed at making banana pumpkin bread together, ending up in a food fight then in the shower to wash each other off.

He filled a place within me that had been empty for some time. Could that be what home felt like?

"Prim? Did you hear me? I asked if you'd heard about tour dates from Mick. What's got you so—Oh," Sara followed my gaze to the men approaching us. "Are you and Robbie...? Girl, we have some catching up to do. Talk to me later."

"Sweetheart, Meadow was asking for you." Charles held out his hand and led her away, leaving me alone with the chief.

"Hey," he said, plunging his hands into his pockets. His greeting was nice but with no kiss on the cheek, no hug, it was cold. He'd gotten too good at being one way in public and one way in private, and I had myself to blame.

"Hi back. Your sister knows how to throw a party. Look at this place."

"Yeah, she goes all out. Can I talk to you for a minute?"

"Of course. Is everything okay?" The way he asked confused me. I'd left his place a couple of hours ago and we seemed better than fine then.

"I have something to show you." He was being awfully mysterious.

I followed him downstream, along a path built at the edge. He kept moving, and I didn't know where he could be taking us, but the walk was beautiful.

Leaves were turning colors, and with the sound of water rushing by, it was like a pocket of tranquility where I could bring a yoga mat and stretch or take a nap.

"Really, how much farther?" The noise of the party was fading behind us. "My heels aren't exactly meant for walking."

"Okay, diva," he chuckled.

"I'm not a diva—" My ankle almost twisted when I stepped on a pebble. "Ow, okay fine, I am. Where are you taking me?"

"Just a little further."

Soon we traveled through an arbor of trees, until we came upon an exquisite sight. An iron bridge connected the two banks of the stream. Ornately designed, the metal swirled in a pattern down one side and up the other, and in the center of it the initials KS for Kissing Springs.

It had to be the most scenic sight in the whole town, but the scowl on Robbie's face concerned me as he scanned the area all around us. Not a soul was in sight.

"What is this place?" I asked.

"A love-lock bridge Dillon had built as a gift to Meadow when he asked her to marry him. You know, with her whole slogan for the town as the Romance Capital of the South, he thought it would add to the town's appeal."

He took a few steps onto the bridge and turned, holding out his hand for me and breaking out the smile that I'd come to recognize as the one he gave only to me.

"Now you hold your hand out? I didn't get much of a greeting when I arrived." I smirked. "What's going on?"

"Come here. Let me make up for it." He pulled me in and captured my lips in several sweet kisses while a gentle breeze blew by. "Better?"

I nodded, and we traveled further across, hand in hand, to the center of the bridge, with the stream flowing beneath us.

"Beautiful," I whispered, as if giving it the reverence it deserved.

"Worth it, right? Now look around you. According to local folklore, this is the most magical place, where lovers connect their souls for life. See, couples come up here, put a lock on the bridge and throw away the key into the water."

"I'm glad you brought me here."

"Me, too. I'm sorry for all the mystery, but I wanted to bring you here and I had to kiss you. Since half the town is at the party, stealing kisses on the love lock bridge with no one around seemed safe for us," he explained with a boyish grin.

*Us...*My heart squeezed at this thing between Robbie and me.

As we leaned over the railing, taking in the view, his arm rested across my shoulders. Protective, possessive, like I belonged to him. And I didn't mind.

I linked my hand with his at my shoulder, eager to stay right here, and forget the party. Maybe someday we'd lock our love on this bridge, too, if we got that far. For now, I enjoyed being in our own special world.

I liked that he didn't pressure me to define what was going on between us yet. Here in this place with Robbie, so hidden and tucked away, I could explore something with a man so different from what I ever had before.

Whether it was the springs, or the bridge, or this dang town, my heart surged with emotions. "Robbie...what if I want something more?"

"More than a kiss?"

I turned into the warmth of his chest and lifted my face to his. "More with us," I whispered. Wrapped in his arms, I pulled his head down to meet my lips. My body melted into his, giving in, opening up to whatever this could be. I didn't need a lock on the bridge to tell me all the possibilities a future with him might hold.

Oblivious to anything or anyone—so caught up with him, the world blurred away—our kisses deepened, reaching a new level of passion right down to my soul.

I didn't hear the clicking noises at first. They could have been birds or wildlife. I was that unaware, focused only on how Robbie was opening up my heart to feel again.

Then I heard footsteps, and they woke me up. The clicking noises were the unmistakable sound of a camera. I startled and parted from Robbie, only to find a man with a professional setup and lens standing at the base of the bridge. Like an uninvited guest ruining my best party, I glared at him.

"Hey, get away from there," Robbie yelled. When the man ran off, he chased after him.

My heart sank. This was exactly what I feared would happen. We'd been so wrapped up in the cocoon of secrecy, and just when I was ready for us to emerge from it together on our terms, someone else forcefully broke it wide open.

I knew how the paparazzi worked, and soon that photo of Robbie and I together would publish. And the entire world would know about *us*...

CHAPTER 16

LOVE IS A F-ING BATTLEFIELD

ROBBIE

ALL HELL BROKE LOOSE in my town thanks to one photo of me kissing a rock star. Plastered everywhere from entertainment news to social media, the headlines were ridiculous.

Rock Star Diva Has a New Date

Prima Puckers Up

Watch Out Bruce, There's a New Sheriff In Town

On the surface, Prima seemed to take it all in stride, but then this was her territory. She was used to this attention. Despite her assurances this would all blow over in a few days, we were a week into this thing and the heat hadn't let up.

The town swelled almost overnight. Members of the paparazzi booked our local hotel and motels, and even the bed-and-breakfast Meadow and I owned was booked solid for the first time since we opened it last year. Those who didn't have a room camped out in their cars on the streets. Strange people with huge lenses on cameras around their necks walked around downtown—and there wasn't a dang thing I could do about any of it.

Sara's sources told her the price of a photo with Prima and I swelled to $100,000. If we were kissing even better—$200k. Shoot, for that price, I told her I'd be willing to release a photo of us myself. She didn't find it funny.

I wasn't laughing either. While the calls and complaints from our townsfolk multiplied as the week went on, so did my headaches. Enough was enough. I called Sheriff Gus Woolsy up at the county for some help.

"Well, if it isn't our local star-studded chief," he answered and roared into his phone. Known for his gut busting laughter, I had to hold my phone away from my ear until it died down.

"Yeah, funny." I rolled my eyes. "Listen, my officers are having a tough time down here. We're being pulled in fifty directions. I wondered if you'd be able to send some of your deputies down to help out for a week or two until all this dies down?"

"Hm. Well, that's an interesting request. You know my deputies only help in emergencies. I wouldn't constitute public displays of affection to be one." He guffawed. I'm glad he was getting a kick out of this at my expense. "Tell you what I'll do, though. If you'll get that mayor of yours to foot the bill, I'll see if some of my guys want overtime pay to come down there and protect your ass."

"Thanks. Big help. I'll be in touch." Asshole. I got off the phone and buried my head in my hands, no better off than I was before that call—Aggravated, tired, and hungry.

People with cameras were literally hunting down Prima and me, so we had to plan every move and continue with the Knights guarding her. I'd spent every night with Prima since Meadow's party, escorting her to and from the studios, sleeping with her and waking up with her in my arms out at Charles' farmhouse.

She insisted we be together, calling me her protector, and there I was, straddling the line between lover and cop.

Things were turning into a fucking battlefield in my head.

By mid-morning, I needed a break. But my normal routine of stopping in at the pie shop to bug Aunt Minnie, have a coffee and a little something for breakfast went disrupted because she'd been so swamped with all these strangers in our town. Several members of her church ladies' group pitched in to help her in what would probably be the highest grossing month the shop had ever had. At least some good could come of it.

Officer Brax poked his head into my office. "Got a call in from the Knights guys on post over at the music studios, saying that something big was happening. Like, *every* person with a camera suddenly converged on the site."

"Shit. I'll head there now. Send every available officer and call in anyone who's off today as well." I grabbed my keys. This was insane. How could I protect her under these conditions? It'd be way too easy for a stalker to gain access to her amid all this chaos.

As I exited the station, I took a deep breath, pushed the door open, and was immediately swarmed with cameras in my face. These guys didn't know when to quit, and the fact that they're protected by the First Amendment made it all that much harder to swallow.

I ignored their questions flung at me, kept mum, and almost made it to my SUV, but a last question hit a nerve as I opened the door, and it got my back up.

"How's it feel to be *fucking* a rock star?" someone shouted.

That one pissed me off, and without thinking, I spat out, "How do you think it feels? Fucking great."

As I locked myself in and started up the vehicle, I realized I'd said it kind of boastfully, like I was showing off. I shook my head. "Dammit, don't let these guys get to you."

When I arrived at the studios, the front entry area was packed, with people covering the sidewalks. I saw Andrew, Dallas, and Foster from the Knights doing an excellent job guarding the entrance. In the alley, where only a few paps sat, I parked and ducked quickly into the building's back door.

Once I entered the studio where Prima and Mutt worked, I watched from behind the glass in the hallway and listened in awe to her new song through the speakers. As a ballad, it not only held an emotionally gripping melody, but she did me in with her voice, all dark and sultry. She told me how she'd poured her heart out into all the lyrics for this album, and I could hear it in every beat.

Her hips swayed, belting out this song of promises broken, lies told, and souls shattered, but toward the end of it, there's a message of hope to love again. Anyone who'd been through a bad breakup would relate. I certainly did. This one would be a chart topper, if my opinion mattered.

With those sexy moves of hers, I couldn't take my eyes off her. Once she spotted me, it was as if we were alone. Every word was sung for me as she stared my way. My cock needed to calm the fuck down, but if I could have crashed into the studio and taken her right there, I would have.

When she finished, she smiled broadly. "Mutt, I need a break." She headed to the control room door, and I swear the producer scowled at me.

"Fuck that. We've hardly made progress this morning," he complained in a gruff voice.

I didn't like the way he talked to her and rushed to the room. I knew from things she told me, while they'd had creative differences, no other producer pushed her to the limit as he did; they created great music together. But it didn't mean he had to be an asshole about it. She opened and closed the door, leaving Mutt behind, and joined me in the hall.

"Is everything okay in there?" I asked.

"Yeah, he's just been a bear all week, and you showing up seems to have aggravated it," she said.

"Do you need me to talk to him, tell him to chill out?"

"No. I can handle Mutt."

I had no doubt she could and turned toward complementing her work. "Awesome song, by the way. I'd say your next number one hit."

She jumped on me, flinging her arms around my neck. I caught her and twirled her around to her squeals of joy. "You think? It's my absolute favorite, but Mutt's campaigning with Mick to cut it from the album altogether."

"No way. Don't do it. Could be your best song ever. Listen to your intuition."

My temptress sucked in my bottom lip in that special way she liked to. "Good advice. You know what my intuition is telling me now? We should go find a quiet room for a quickie."

"I love your line of thinking, darling, but considering the precarious situation with the paparazzi going on outside, I need to be on alert for anything." I put her feet back on the ground.

"I know. It's so weird with so many of them out there, like they know something's going to happen today and they don't want to miss it." Her words made the hairs stand on the back of my neck.

"I sure hope not. The town's already in an uproar," I said just as the elevator dinged and opened behind me.

Prima gasped as its occupant came into view down the hall. "Bruce? What the *hell* are you doing here?" She cried, raising her voice.

I did an about face to find an Italian-looking dude strutting down the hall toward us, complete with what was surely a custom-made pinstriped suit.

Mutt flung open the door to the studio control room, laying eyes on him as well. "Well, this day just got more interesting." He crossed his arms and leaned against the doorjamb.

Fuck me. What timing for her ex to show up? He pointed my way. "So, *you're* the man fucking my wife."

"Excuse me?" Prima's face reddened as she stepped in front of me with her fists at her sides. "*Ex-wife*. Don't *ever* forget the ex. We're divorced, remember?"

I admired her bravery, but in this circumstance, I could take him down with one punch.

"I've been following you, and watching you." The man who used to share Prima's bed got too damn close to her for my tastes. "There's no way this guy will ever measure up to me. Come back to me, sweetie."

That got my attention. I squinted at him. "Following her? Exactly how long have you been in Kissing Springs?" I was ten seconds away from hauling his ass down to the station for questioning.

"A few days. Enough to know Prima would never be happy in this podunk town."

She scoffed. "You don't know me anymore."

Mutt barged in. "Wait, has it been you sending threatening messages to Prima? She has a stalker, and it's getting serious."

I didn't appreciate Mutt's interference to question Bruce. "Can you account for your whereabouts for the past few weeks?"

"My god. You think *I'd* do something like that?" Bruce's face looked stricken, but I was sure it was all an act. The guy seemed faker than fake. This was the type of man Prima went for before me?

He took another step too close to her and dared place a hand on her arm. "I would *never*...In fact, Prima, if you need a place to hide out, come back with me to my villa in the Caymans."

She brushed his hand off. Good girl. "And let you siphon my money again? No thanks. I have a better idea. Why don't you give me back the money you stole?"

"See, that's where we differ. I prefer the word *investment*. I sunk it all into my new venture, BM Productions. I'm managing some fresh music groups now, and I'd love to have you back."

"I would *never*—" she started.

I stepped in front of her. "Look, man, you need to come down to the station with me and answer a few questions about your whereabouts."

"I'm staying right here, talking to my wife." His face reddened as he raised his voice.

"Harassing is more like it, a cousin to stalking. You can come peacefully or I can handcuff you. Your choice."

He raised his voice and spoke over my shoulder to Prima. "You have the local sheriff looking into the stalker? Let me hire you a top-notch private eye."

"Chief of Police. And I'm handling the investigation just fine." I was shouting now, too.

"I can see that...and so can a billion other people." He held up his phone in my face, showing the picture of her and me kissing on the bridge.

We almost came to fists over that as I lost my cool and scowled nose to nose with him. As a cop, I'd wait for him to attack so I could arrest him for assaulting me. As a man, I was holding myself back from taking that first punch.

"Stop it, all of you. Enough." Prima screamed and ran down the hall. Not waiting for the elevator, she headed down the stairs.

Bruce was quicker and rushed after her. Mutt grabbed my shoulder, holding me back. I almost slugged him.

"Let them work it out. Besides, haven't you done enough? Or maybe not enough? How hard can it be to investigate a stalker?" He snickered.

"What the fuck would you know about it? Think you can do my job?"

"I think you're in over your head, not only with the case, but with Prima, too."

"Shut the fuck up, man." I started walking away.

"What do you think will happen when this is all over? You think she's going to stick around here in this small town? Hell no. Prima is a superstar. She'll leave you behind in her dust, just like all the others before you. I've seen it happen. Be prepared for heartbreak." He backed up into the control room and slammed the door.

I ran down the hall and tried to put his words out of my head. But they echoed the depths of my fears. I let myself get too close to this case, to her, and I was losing control.

CHAPTER 17

STRONGER THAN THIS

PRIMA

"PRIMA, STOP!" Bruce yelled from the flight of stairs above me. I made it to the second floor and kicked off my heels, going the rest of the way barefoot.

"Stop. I just want to talk." There was no way—He was the last person on Earth I wanted a conversation with.

At the bottom, I swung open the door to the lobby of the old building and made it to the front entrance. Outside the windows, paparazzi people spotted me and went ballistic, their camera flashes popping off one after the other. The security guards at the door had a tough time holding them back and were almost being smashed against the glass.

Trapped between Bruce behind me and the cameras in front of me, the walls started closing in. My heart raced and I couldn't breathe, like I was back in that tiny room my mother locked me in, having no control.

No, this couldn't be my life. I had to fight.

I turned, but ran right into Bruce's chest. He caught me up. "Let me go. I don't need you."

"No, but I need you. I've been lost without you. I realize the error of my ways. Please, come back to me, Prima. We'll work things out." He pulled me into him, strong, almost like Robbie, or maybe it was me, weakening by the second.

The crowd outside turned ugly, sounding like an angry mob as shouts between the guards and people increased. The walls were getting closer and closer, and I could feel myself beginning to hyperventilate.

"We need to get out of here. This isn't safe for you. Come with me," he said, and with his hand tightening around my arm, he rushed us through the lobby. But this wasn't right; Robbie was my protector, not him.

"I can't go with you. I don't—"

"Sh. Babe, we can talk in the car." We burst through the back door, but some paparazzi were camped out there, too, and they went nuts seeing us.

I needed to escape all this, calm down, and think straight. A black car was waiting, running in the alley, and his driver held the door for us. I launched in head first and Bruce followed. But then he turned to the cameras and spoke.

"Prima and I are reconciling. Please, give us some space."

My jaw dropped. That brought me to my senses. As soon as he was in and the car pulled away, I gave him hell.

"Oh my God! You set this all up and alerted the paps so they'd see us together, didn't you?"

He answered with a sly smile. "Any publicity is good publicity, right? I have a new business and need to raise my profile so I can attract new stars to manage. This stunt was perfect."

What was I doing still sitting here? I was stronger than this. "You asshole. We're *not* reconciling."

"Prima, I love you. Time to stop the charade."

"The only person you love is yourself. Driver, pullover. I'm getting out." The car kept moving. Bruce snickered.

"All right. You've had your fun. I let you have your little divorce and your breakdown in a small town. Now it's time to get back to work. You're coming with me and we're going to work this out."

"Like hell we are. For all I know, you could be the stalker and be intending to kill me. Driver, pull the fuck over." I slapped the door.

Bruce pushed a button for the glass partition to separate us from him. "Why the hell would I kill you or hurt you? Your star power is worth more to me alive than dead."

"Screw you. There's no way I'm going back to you and the life we had. You used me, Bruce. You manipulated my career for years and hid all my money away. *My* money that I earned with every word I sang and every script I had to memorize."

"Oh, don't act all innocent. You loved the fame you gained under my control. *I* worked hard to make it happen for us. And fortune? Shit, babe, I kept you in style. You were well provided for, and what thanks did I get? You stopped acting the parts well, couldn't write a note of music, and left us in a pile of debt. You even stopped fucking me. So yeah, I tucked money away—to prepare for your comeback. And look at you...on your way back up, just like I predicted."

What an asshole—what did I ever see in him? This was possibly the best therapy session ever, as I finally saw the real Bruce. "That's because *you* worked me to the bone, and you made a series of poor decisions for my career. I was tired and needed a break, but you wouldn't listen, and you damn sure weren't letting me have any say in my movie roles or my music."

"Fine. You looking for someone to blame, sweetheart? Sure, I'll take the heat. Just shut the fuck up. We're leaving this town and getting *our* career back in line."

I couldn't do this anymore with him, fighting the same battle over and over and never winning. Just like before, I needed to get out from under his control and to get far away from him for my sanity, for my health.

He started spouting off all the mistakes he thought I made in this deal with Mick to produce my music, and I only half-listened. Why did I leave Robbie? I could be with him now, in the safety of his arms, not sitting in a car with my lunatic ex-husband.

"I'll take over and have a little chat with Mick. You'll go out on tour, make us a shit ton of money. We'll find your next movie to star in, something huge, and we'll be back on track."

We came to a stop sign in front of the grocery store. I spied all the people doing their shopping, carrying on with their average routines, not worried about critics or the pressures of stardom. For a while, I was part of it, in Robbie's arms, leading a somewhat normal life, and I liked it there with him.

Without a doubt in my heart, I knew I belonged there, not in this car. If only I could turn back time and try again. Or would I go even further back, to the beginning, to the one place in time where I faced a fork in the road—when I was Melody? Knowing what I knew now, would I stand up for myself, refusing for Mom to turn me into Prima?

"Actually, all the publicity and attention you've gained while divorcing me, plus your little tryst with the officer, serves us well," Bruce continued, full of himself and his words. I was so sick of him. "As it turns out, your star is on the rise again. I even have offers flooding in for your appearances and movies. Well done, babe."

"No, it's over between us, and I'll never go back." Before the car rolled through the stop sign, I saw my chance. I opened the door and scrambled out, running for the store, not daring to look back.

Once inside, I kept moving forward, one foot in front of the other, leaving the past behind, and praying Bruce wasn't following me. When I reached the back area of the store, I didn't see any employees around, but there was a huge walk-in cooler, perfect to hide in.

Tucked in behind some boxes, after having moved some other boxes in front of me, I waited, listening, hoping no one would find me here. I checked my phone, but had no service inside this cold chamber, but no matter how much my skin shivered, I wouldn't dare move.

Eventually, my heart calmed down, and my breathing regulated. From time to time, employees would come in and grab a box, but no one knew I was there. After a couple of hours, when I figured enough time had lapsed, it took all the bravery I could muster to step out of the cooler.

A big truck was sitting at the dock waiting to be unloaded, and I snuck out. Finally, outside behind a dumpster, I called the one person in my life that would always be there for me —the one person I could trust, even more than Robbie.

Sara picked up on the first ring. "Oh my God, Prima. Where are you? We're all worried."

"I need help. Can you come get me?"

Within the hour, a sleek sports car I recognized as one of Charles' cars from his garage came screeching to a halt in front of the dumpsters. The door opened and Robbie popped out. "Prima?"

"I'm here!" I left my crouching position and ran toward him. He ran too, and we collided in the middle, where he picked me up and spun me around, holding me tight in his arms. This feeling with him meant everything to me—security, promises, and home.

"Thank fuck, you're all right," his words buried in my hair.

"Robbie, it was so terrible," I cried, not caring at all if I looked weak, and let the tears fall.

He put me down and smoothed away each drop from my cheeks. I could see a million questions in his eyes and hoped I had an answer for each one. "Safety first. Let's get you out of here."

Only when we were buckled in and well on our way did we talk. "Where are we going?"

"Off-grid to a cabin for a couple of days to let all this nonsense die down. Mick and your sister are the only two who know."

We headed out of town on a road I hadn't yet been on. I looked behind us a few times, relieved no one followed.

"Don't worry. Sara had the brilliant idea to walk downtown with me and draw the paps away. They went crazy when we hugged, then she ducked into my SUV with Charles behind the wheel, while I drove off with this."

"Ah, yes. That was a trick we used many times in L.A. She's so smart." Tears threatened my eyes again. I loved my sister to pieces, and the next time I saw her I'd lavish her with hugs for always coming through for me.

"I guess I never realized before how much you two really look similar, enough to fool people who don't know you well, anyway." His hand landed on my thigh and he squeezed it, leaving it there.

"That won't work much longer, with twins growing in her belly." I smiled, laced my fingers with his and, in his presence, I finally felt able to breathe again. The tightness in my heart I'd experienced all day left me after a cleansing breath in and out.

The change of scenery out the window appealed. We were headed into the hills, and the houses thinned out. With the fall leaves changing colors on the trees, it was a beautiful sight. Autumn was suddenly my favorite season.

"So, what happened out there? Are you ready to talk? Did Bruce try to hurt you?" His pained expression and jaw clenching made me realize what my disappearing did to him. Robbie cared for me. There was no denying that. "Do you believe he's the one who's been stalking you?"

"No, definitely not the stalker. Just a pain in my ass." I told him every detail of the entire story and ended with an apology. "I'm so sorry, Robbie."

"What the hell? You have nothing to be sorry for."

"I should have stayed with you at the studio. I'm sure somehow, someway, we'd have figured out how to force Bruce to leave."

"Hey, you did what you had to do to get away from an uncomfortable situation. It's understandable. Don't beat yourself up for it."

"I wonder where he is now?"

"While we were all out looking for you, one of the Knights spotted him and followed him. They'll keep on him and report on his whereabouts. But believe me, there's no way he's getting within an inch of you again. Not while you're in my town." He brought my hand to his lips and kissed my knuckles.

"You can't be with me all the time, though."

"You should consider getting a restraining order against Bruce, and maybe your mother, too. That would help."

"And, um...what happens when I'm not in your town?" The question hung between us, waiting for answers neither of us had. He was quiet for a minute and I worried for us, that I'd put him on the spot, until he finally answered.

"Guess that's something we'll have time to figure out in the next couple of days. We still have a little way to go yet. You must be exhausted. Here, lean back, try to nap."

He pulled some shoes and a garment out of the backseat— his KSPD sweatshirt. I covered my body with it, surrounded by the scent of him, wrapped in the comfort of it like it was his own arms.

He was right. Too tired to think anymore, I closed my eyes, shutting out the world for only a little while, hoping it would do me good.

CHAPTER 18

I'M THE ONLY ONE FOR YOU

ROBBIE

THE FACE of an angel slept in the seat beside me. We'd come so far this fall, from secret lovers to everything out in the open to...I didn't know what, now. Where did we stand after all this?

The rambling route out into the hills halfway between Kissing Springs and Louisville did me good; a country drive always had that effect on me. On the open road, I could think clearer and contemplate life.

Only this afternoon, just to be safe, I doubled back a few miles here and there, ensuring I wasn't followed. The view and the country station playing softly on my radio kept me company while Prima napped.

"And now, we have a special treat for y'all." The radio disc jockey broke through the music. "Country music star Nicoletta is joining us live over the phone. I hear this is your first interview since having your baby?"

"Yes. We're so blessed with our sweet baby girl. My husband says we'll keep trying until we get a boy," she said with a twang in her voice that was cheerful.

The DJ chuckled. "Well, thanks for being here today to debut your latest single. Tell us about it."

"I'd be happy to. It's a sweet little tune written by a new songwriting friend of mine, Sara Simms. She writes lovely songs about family and the people that matter most to you."

I listened to a bit of it, happy for Sara to have found success. After falling for Charles and finding out they would be expecting, she carved a new life for herself here, content to stay and raise a family. Since landing in Kissing Springs and working with Wild Horses Music, she'd come into her own, and found her version of success.

She was lovely—but what she saw in Charles Montgomery, I couldn't comprehend. Although maybe she was just what he needed to ground him and keep him lawful. I could only hope. Aw hell, a part of me always cheered when two people found love, even if it was Charles.

One thing I was certain of, Sara and Prima were total opposites. Sara managed to find a home here and stay, but something told me Prima would be harder to hold on to. Since we started, I knew she was a wild thing, and I'd be taking my chances if I took a ride with her.

Maybe a part of me foolishly thought I could tame her. With more time, perhaps I could. Her big concert in town was coming up. Then what after that?

I finally turned off the main road, down an overgrown path no one had tended to in some time. I woke up Prima by squeezing her thigh. "Hey, darling, wake up."

"Mm. Okay." She sat upright, rubbing her eyes. It'd been some time since I was here, so I didn't know what we'd find, but hopefully something to eat and a bed at least.

Way back in, the trees eventually parted enough for a small cabin to appear. I parked in front, but looked around before moving. The rustic siding on the house needed repair here and there. Otherwise, it looked clean and kempt, the only sign of life from the smoke rising out of the chimney.

"Who lives here?" she asked.

"Remember, I told you about Mac? This is his place, and the safest place I know to keep you for a couple of days."

We got out, and I approached the door and knocked. When it creaked open, an old man with a long gray beard and hair stood there, in clothes that hung off of him, leaning on a walking stick made of wood. I almost didn't recognize him.

He glanced me up and down. "Robbie? That you?"

"Hi Mac. It's been a while. This is Prima."

"So nice to meet you. Robbie speaks highly of you." She hooked her hand through my arm.

"Oh, I don't know if I've earned it, but he's always been a good guy," he chuckled.

"Mac, we need a place to stay for a couple of days. I was hoping you could put us up."

"Stay or hide out?"

I traded glances with Prima. "Little bit of both."

"Come on in then. I fired up the stove for the night, about to make supper, and just put the kettle on. We'll have some tea and you can tell me all about it. I've been a little lonely lately, so lucky for you, I could use a good story."

We entered the cabin, and I found it cozy, as usual. He'd become a minimalist, turning to nature in his older years, long ago having used my help and gotten rid of a lot of junk. I always felt at peace here, sequestered away from the world.

Prima looked around and I was glad she didn't snub her nose at the rustic surroundings. She'd probably never known anyone who lived off-grid a day in her life.

He hobbled over to his kitchen and reached up into a cupboard for two more mugs.

From the looks of him, would he be able to live here much longer on his own? "Need help?"

"Bah," he brushed me off. Mac was always a tough guy, but getting up in age, and I worried.

He tossed two tea bags on an old, slender farmhouse table and motioned for us to sit. While we watched him quickly whip together some eggs, bacon, and potatoes, I held Prima's hand, squeezing it now and then for reassurance.

The smells permeated around us, like a good fall camp-out, when he finally set down each plateful. "Now, tell me all the news."

I started filling him in, and Prima added details here and there. Mac's old lawman's eyes would gleam now and then, especially about the stalker case.

He laughed hoarsely when we finished, with a bemused look on his face. "Yep, guess I'm glad I retired years ago. I don't have the energy to chase all the nonsense anymore."

"Doesn't matter your age. I could still use a good man like you on my force," I said.

Stroking his beard, he sat quietly for a moment. I shared so many memories with him, with his daughter, and his family. Years that I wouldn't trade, even now. The respect I had for him couldn't be measured. My heart almost broke seeing him like this, old, sad, rundown.

"Welp, the sun's going down. How about you help me light the lanterns, Robbie? And, pretty lady, come with me. We'll find some fresh linens for the bed so you can have a rest. I have some things to talk with Robbie about, just old man crap you'll find boring as hell."

He insisted we take the bed, and he'd sleep out in his old truck and nothing I could say would change his mind. While he waited for me on the porch, I watched Prima undress, then I tucked her in, stuffing an extra blanket all around her. She'd been more quiet than usual all evening.

"I know these aren't exactly the five star accommodations you're used to."

"No, but it's cozy enough. The bed is surprisingly comfortable. You may not know this, but when Sara and I were younger, we spent most of every summer in a camper with our mother, driving town to town for me to perform at every county fair or wherever she could book us. Honestly, as hard as Mom was on us, those summers with Sara were some of my favorite times."

"Are you saying there's a little bit of small town in you yet?" The smile on my face widened. Nothing would make me happier than to hear it.

"Maybe." Her coy smile almost kept me there in bed with her. "Now, go talk to Mac. I'll be right here waiting for you to come back and keep me warm."

I planted a kiss on her forehead. "Oh, I have some ways to keep you nice and warm all night." I left her and meandered in the dim lantern light around the kitchen. I knew where he kept his bottles of alcohol—and his moonshine.

I opted for a good old bottle of Kentucky bourbon, and took a couple of glasses out to the porch. Mac sat there, smoking, rocking in a chair, and I took up next to him in another.

The night was chilled and a cool breeze kicked up as we drank. I was glad to have some time alone with him.

"There's more news. I didn't want to get into it with Prima there." I rocked a little and continued. "The Brown Jug Bar burned down, and during the cleanup, they discovered the remains of Fannie Boyd's body buried under the old foundation."

His rocking chair halted, the creaking stopped, and the silence was almost deafening. "I picked up a newspaper some campers threw out on a trail in the hills and saw. Do you have any idea how she got there?"

"Not a single clue. I figured you or Ogden Montgomery would know, but he left town."

He snuffed out his cigarette and promptly lit another. His smoking was the only thing that ever bothered me about him and I'd been after him to quit for years.

He didn't speak for a while, and I didn't push it, while the cigarette in his fingers became almost entirely a long cylinder of ashes. I almost wondered if he was asleep. A quick glance showed his eyes were wide open.

"Robbie, there are some things that are better left in the past." He stared out into the dark with a horrified look on his face. I didn't even want to know what that meant, but he didn't appear well. Following his gaze to his truck, which was backed up near the porch, I realized the back of it was packed.

"Are you heading somewhere?"

"Yep." He crushed that cig in his ashtray. "I'm going on my final hunting trip."

"Final?"

"I have the big C, Robbie. I don't have much longer."

What the—I felt as if part of my world shattered. I should have come to visit him more often. The man who inspired so much of my life sat here alone, fighting a disease with no cure.

"Mac, I'm so sorry."

"Don't be. I'm fine with it. I've had a hell of a life, but I refuse to die in some hospital somewhere. Nope. A few months from now, send out your buddies from Search and Rescue to find me. You know where all my favorite hunting spots are."

"Jeezus, I wish I'd known." Sick to my stomach, I bent over, with my elbows on my knees, and tried to contain my heartache.

"Don't feel sorry for me. I've lived one helluva life. I served my community as an officer and chief for forty years, and tried to leave it in your very capable hands. You know I loved my wife deeply, and my daughters, too. But I've also known deep loss. It's been a full life and I have no regrets. But you —" He choked up. "You were like a son to me."

I stood and grabbed up his thin body and held onto him tight, choking back the tears. "No, Mac. This can't be. Come to Kissing Springs with me. I'll do what I can to keep you comfortable."

"Bah. My mind is set." He slapped my back a few times, then slumped into the chair after I released him. I fought to control the emotions swarming me.

"Is there anything I can do for you?"

"First of all, after I go, you'll find some letters in the top drawer of my desk. Some to send to my wife and children."

I shook my head, knowing there wasn't a damn thing I could do to change his stubborn mind.

"Second, do me a favor? Be happy and love hard. I was always sad that things didn't work out between you and my daughter. But that woman in there? She looks like she needs a good man in her life, so be the rock for her."

Getting advice from the man who was my mentor at work and in life was the last thing I thought would happen tonight. I couldn't go to sleep now, not after this.

We stayed up for hours, drinking and reminiscing, laughing and talking, and before I knew it, the sun was rising, and my time with Mac expired way too soon.

"Welp. I best get going." He used his cane to help him stand.

"Mac, wait. Take the bed. Stay another day."

"Bah. I'm set with my plans. I'm going to sleep a few hours before I hit the road." He hobbled down the porch steps to his truck.

"I'll clear my schedule and come with you. Give me a day to catch up." I followed him.

At his truck, he paused. "Son, you have a life to live. Don't follow mine into death. You're a good man. Now go on, you've left your gal alone too long. Go warm her up." With a wink, he got into the driver's side and covered himself with some blankets.

My feet were glued to the spot, as I watched him quickly drift off to sleep. Gutted, the man who I revered would soon be gone from my life forever, and I knew he was too stubborn to let me change his mind.

I stumbled through the cabin and to the bed where Prima slept, distraught and dealing with all these feelings. There was a time about a year ago I thought I'd end up like Mac, alone with no one. Now, as I undressed and crawled in next to her, I had someone, but for how long?

She was a rock star, only temporarily in Kissing Springs, about to shoot off into orbit again the minute her new album released. How could I compete with the call of the stage, with the fans who loved her? How could I make her see I was the only one for her?

CHAPTER 19

TAKE FROM ME ALL OF MY PAIN

ROBBIE

THE MORNING SUNLIGHT glared through Mac's threadbare curtains. I groaned and had hardly slept, dazed and upset about everything. Prima stirred and turned into me, making the bed creak. She brushed my lips, but I wanted much more. All of her, to claim her, not letting her get away.

She moaned, caressing my cock, getting it nice and thick. She's what I needed right now to soothe my soul, to make me forget the hurt in my heart left there by Mac. But the concert she'd been preparing for would happen soon, and then what—a tour? Where would that leave us?

I snaked a hand down between us, finding her wet center, searching through her folds, and strummed her clit. "Been dreaming of me?"

"Yes. You stayed out all night. I thought you guys would never stop talking. Is everything all right?"

I couldn't speak without choking up, so instead I pressed her back onto the bed, and settled between her legs. I lined up to her seam, teasing her clit, getting my cock slick, finding the entrance.

Slowly, I pushed in, inch by inch, taking my sweet time with this—making love. Her hands smoothed down my back and our lips connected. A million kisses. Sweet heat. Everything shared between us. Vulnerable to these hazy feelings, only she could fill the hole in my heart.

But a dozen worries hit me all at once, taking me away from this bliss with her in bed, until her palms framed my cheeks. "Where are you right now? What's going on?"

With the sunlight hitting her eyes, turning them bright green, I had a brilliant place to focus, and I knew... "Mellie, everything has been crazy, but I think I'm falling for you."

I claimed her lips and deepened my strokes, and if she wasn't in the same place as me, it was fine. I could live with that. It was better that I told her, let her know where I stood, than to keep it hidden away.

She came up for air and gasped. "Robbie...My past has been a mess, and I look ahead and it's still a big huge hot mess, but right here with you, everything is clear."

"Then tell me." I continued my deep strokes, and added my thumb and finger, applying pressure to her clit.

"I'm falling, too."

My pace increased, but I had to hear one more thing from her lips. "Tell me I'm the only one for you."

"Don't you know? You've been mine from the beginning. Oh, that sounds like a fantastic song lyric. You're so good for me." Her words, her smile, took from me all my pain.

I pushed her arms above her head and laced our fingers together. Our bodies and souls connected with each thrust, deeper and deeper, and I didn't stop until I had poured everything I had into her. Every hope from the past, every dream for the future, every emotion. They belonged to her now.

Mac was gone when we finally got up. I scrounged around the cabin's kitchen for food and coffee. I could tell Mac had been planning his exit from life for a while because provisions were scarce. There were just a few pieces of wood left to light up the stove for coffee, and two eggs. It's surprising he had enough to make us eggs and bacon the night before.

I shook off thoughts of him, trying to focus on what Prima and I needed. After checking the weather forecast on my phone, looked like some chilly fall wind headed our way overnight.

Coming out to the cabin wasn't such a great idea after all, but with how fast everything happened, I had little time to prepare. Had I known I'd be taking her away from Kissing Springs, I'd have packed properly.

Had I known last night would be my final visit with Mac, I'd have showed up a week ago.

I cooked the eggs and coffee up for us on the wood-fired stove, and brought it out to the porch where she was rocking in a chair, bundled up in a blanket despite also wearing my sweatshirt.

"Here we go. Breakfast in the wild. Sorry, but it's all Mac had left."

She at least didn't make any comments or scrunched up faces while eating and drinking.

To me, everything tasted like crap, soured mostly due to my heart hurting, and after I'd finished I had to laugh, teasing her. "I'll bet you'd eat an entire cinnamon roll from Aunt Minnie's now."

She followed me into the joke, nodding excessively. "Hell yeah. Screw the dress for my concert. Right now, carbs laced with cream cheese frosting would be perfect."

It felt good to joke around, to lighten the mood. But pretty quickly, I was right back where I was, down again. She noticed.

"Hey, Mr. Sunshine. Mind telling me what's going on in that head of yours?"

"Mac's gone and not coming back." I spilled all the details from my conversation with him, as we rocked in the chairs on the porch side by side, holding hands between. Occasionally, I'd pause, trying to keep it together, trying to remain strong in front of her. Finally, she shifted out of her seat and planted herself across my lap.

"Chief, you don't have to hold back for me. I know you're a very strong man, but you don't have to be all the time. I see you and I'm here for you." She touched me with her words more than I could ever express. I kissed her for that.

"Thanks. I'll be all right. He made his last wishes known and I'll follow through. The grieving process will suck, but eventually, I'll be fine."

A stiff wind kicked up around us, blowing her hair back. She shrunk inside the blanket. "Brrr."

I snuggled her tighter into me and grimaced. "You've been a real trooper through all of this, but with little firewood and no food, I think we better head back to town today. Unless you care to watch me chop wood and kill small critters."

"Oh, thank God." She jumped up from my lap. "I mean, I like this place, don't get me wrong. With some TLC, it could make a great getaway cabin. But yeah, I'm totally ready to head back to civilization now."

I couldn't help but smile at the diva inside of her. It's a part of what made Prima tick, and I wouldn't want to change her for the world. Still, her life as a star versus mine was vastly different. "Back to the civilization where all the people with cameras are hunting us down? Don't you get tired of it?"

Her shoulders drooped. "I do, but it comes with the job. I've learned how to deal with it over the years. Of course, right now it's a little excessive, so you're seeing a very extreme version of my life, having to hide from the cameras until this all passes."

"Guess so." I hauled my ass up off the rocking chair and went inside to gather our things.

"Trust me, normally it's not that big of a deal. I can walk down Melrose Avenue in L.A., and maybe a dozen people recognize me and want to take a picture or have an autograph. Actually, here it's been nice, because hardly anyone bothers me at all. I think only one or two people have asked for my autograph."

"So, are you saying you like it here?" I fished for her thoughts and paced over to Mac's desk. The last things I needed to grab before we left were those letters he talked about.

"It really surprised me, but yeah, I think I do. You know…" she paused and joined me at the desk. "Sara's here now. She's about to have babies and I'll be an auntie. She's the only family I have, so maybe, I don't know…Maybe I'll stay."

My head snapped to hers, trying to use all my years in police work to gauge her expression, to find the sincerity in what she was saying, before I got my hopes up. "Seriously?"

"Yeah. Of course, I'll have to fly out for appearances and tour dates and such, but I think Kissing Springs would make a nice home base."

The future of us formulated in my head. I could have her here with me some of the time, while she'd be gone for the rest. What an interesting predicament, to want all of her for me, but to compete for her time. As if she were married to her life as a rock star, and I'd be her part-time lover.

Old wounds came back from when my ex cheated on me. I didn't like it then, but now, to tame this wild woman would mean putting up with being second best.

It all wasn't sitting well with me, but then a call came in on her phone. "It's Sara. Let me put her on speaker. Hey sis, Robbie and I are at this rustic little cabin out in the middle of nowhere."

"Oh good. I knew he'd take you someplace safe. But sweetie, I hate to tell you this. Another email arrived from the stalker."

"Oh no. What does it say about me this time?"

"It's a threat again, but not for you. For Robbie."

What? My ears perked up. "Sara, I'm listening. Can you send a copy to Prima's phone?" I barked.

"Will do. Right away."

"Okay. We're heading back there to your place today. See you in a little while," Prima said, then clicked off. "Now they're threatening you? I'm so sorry I ever brought you into this. If we hadn't gotten involved—"

I wrapped my arms around her. "Hey, don't be sorry. I'm not. You had no idea this would escalate. Go on out to the truck. I'll be right behind you."

I quickly fished everything out of Mac's desk. A whole pile of stuff included the letters to his family, an envelope marked last will and testament, a mortgage for this place, and pre-paid burial services. At the bottom of the pile, one envelope was left.

I stared at Mac's scribbled writing:

Robbie: All the answers you seek.

Scowling, I almost ripped the envelope open, but my heart ached and I wasn't ready to deal with whatever he wrote inside. Instead, I stuffed all of it I into a bag I found from under the kitchen sink, then we headed to my car.

After we buckled in, Prima got Sara's email and clicked and enlarged the photo on the screen. Viewing a copy of the photo of Prima and me kissing on the bridge, my jaw clenched and my knuckles turned white on the steering wheel.

The warning came to me this time from some sicko who dared send it. Same as before, the white paper with black block lettering appeared. This time with the words: *STAY AWAY FROM HER OR ELSE YOU'LL BE SORRY.*

CHAPTER 20

HERE'S SOMETHING TO TALK ABOUT

PRIMA

"GREAT JOB, guys. I think we're ready," I addressed the band to close out our final rehearsal. We'd practiced the concert playlist all week, including some of my greatest hits, plus all the new songs.

A lump in my throat caught there. It'd been a mad rush to the finish all week, all while being on guard against some weirdo threatening me and Robbie.

My hairdresser, makeup and costume artists and my entire wardrobe for the concert all arrived on time, and fit me perfectly. This despite Robbie bringing me cinnamon rolls to eat every damn day, but I loved his attention.

The pyrotechnic guys did what they could within the confines of the classic Boyd Theater, but they'd be very effective at getting the crowd rocking. With the sound check complete, the lights on point, and my choreography arranged, I had a hand in managing it all, and finally, everything was ready for the biggest concert of my life.

Big was a relative term. I've played larger venues than this, selling over a hundred thousand tickets in minutes, but in terms of creating something all mine, this concert in Kissing Springs was bigger and meant so much more. I couldn't be prouder of what I'd accomplished in such a short time.

"Actually, I think you should do that third number again. The band sounded okay, but you were off, Prima," Mutt complained, being a total downer.

He'd been like that all week, grumpy as hell, bitching and moaning about things, and I was over it. We'd wrapped up the production on the album earlier this week, and all he did was mull about and scowl.

"Nope, I'm done. I'll pull it off in concert just fine. Tonight, my throat needs to rest." I glared at him.

"The queen has spoken. That's a wrap," said Gregor, my drummer, playing some cymbals to cue the end.

Damian, my bass player, set up his instrument, ready for the next day. "Yep, time to party. Where's the nearest bar?"

"I'd like to find some authentic local Kentucky bourbon," Cruise, my guitar player, announced. The others in the band agreed.

"The best place for that would be Lockland's Distillery," Robbie called, approaching from the aisle. Thanks to the threat of violence against a police officer from the stalker, the sheriff finally took this seriously and sent a team of deputies to help. Robbie had been coordinating things between them, police, and the Knights all week.

He also helped Dillon, Charles, and Meadow with other preparations for the sold out show, which would bring an influx of five thousand people into Main Street and the Boyd Theater for Halloween. It warmed my heart that fans would pay a premium price for these exclusive tickets for one of my first concerts in years.

Between my profit on the concert, plus a plethora of Prima merchandise, and of course, my new album available tomorrow, I should be back on top, with my career once again on a solid path.

"My hero," I yelled to Robbie. I put my complete trust and faith in him, that he had it all covered, that I'd be safe. He promised he'd be the one personally watching over me, standing just a few feet away in the wings throughout the entire concert. I couldn't wait to have him there.

I practically jumped from the stage into his arms, and with the biggest rush because everything was perfect, I couldn't help but tell him exactly how I felt. "I love you." Robbie had become my lifeline, my rock, grounding me, preventing me from lonely days and nights. I never wanted another day where he wasn't in my life.

"And I love you, my wild woman. Good thing I caught you. You wouldn't want to break a leg before the actual concert, now would you?" He laughed.

"Doesn't matter. I'm so excited to rock the stage tomorrow night, I'd do it limping with a cast on."

"Yeah, just what your fans want to see," Mutt rudely remarked nearby. That was it. I was done with him.

"What is your problem? All week you've been like this, yucking on my yum." I slid down Robbie's body to stand.

Mutt glared first at me, then at Robbie, then back at me. "I think I've had enough of the Prima show. I'm leaving this town."

"Leaving? I thought you'd be happy with the music we created, that you'd want to see the looks on fans' faces when they hear it all tomorrow for the first time. You've been amazing in producing my album, but now you need to chill and just enjoy the show."

"Amazing?" He glared harshly over at Robbie. "Apparently not amazing enough."

"What the hell are you talking about?"

"Nothing. Excuse me, I'll go drown myself in some bourbon now. Would that make you happy?"

I paced closer to him. "Sure, if it'll lighten up this negative mood you've been in."

"Whatever, Prima," he called as he hustled up the aisle.

The nerve of him, I huffed, watching him disappear out the doors.

"Are you okay?" Robbie asked, coming up behind me, placing a possessive hand at the lower part of my back.

"Sure. I'm not going to let him ruin our night together." We'd practically created a fortress out of Charles' home since we returned from the cabin, with it being guarded around the clock for our protection.

Sara, Charles, and the girls went to stay at Minnie's for the week, calling it a little vacation for Grace and Hope to think of it as fun, while Robbie and I slept in my room at Charles' house each night in my bed together.

Later that night, after a nice candlelit dinner Robbie cooked in my honor, we made love, lingering in the sweet, deep passion we'd built for each other little by little all season. Now, sprawled across his chest and torso, my one leg draped over his leg, his fingertips softly caressed my back.

"What's in that head of yours, chief?" He was quiet, more than usual.

"Tomorrow, at the concert, I hope it all goes smoothly. I want that for you."

I believed I'd gotten to know Robbie pretty well in such a short time, and recognized a pinch of worry in his voice.

"Why wouldn't it? Mick, Dillon, and I have planned every detail of the concert with some of the best people in the industry paid to make this thing the best it can be. You've handled all the security arrangements. We've considered any potential issues and strategized accordingly."

"But there's one unknown I can't predict and that's whoever this stalker is. What if I lose you tomorrow because of someone beyond my control?"

"Hey," I lifted up on my elbow and brought a hand to his cheek. His bright blue eyes stared back at me, loving, concerned. "We got this. Whatever happens, we'll make it through, because I love you, Robbie. And that has to count for something."

He caressed my cheek with the back of his hand. "Yes, it does. And I love you, Mellie. But after..." He left that hanging in the air. I understood what he was getting at, but I had tunnel vision for the concert and couldn't quite see beyond that yet.

"After...I'll still be here. This will be my new home base, remember? Whatever Mick is arranging for my publicity and tour for the new album, I can fly out, but always return. Right here." I patted and placed my palm over his heart. "If you have room for me to move in and stay, that is."

"If we're talking about room in my heart, darling, I have plenty. If we're talking about a place to live together, the cottage doesn't have the closet space I suspect you'll need."

"Oh, yeah, well think of how much fun it'll be to find a new place together. Some place we can call our own." We laughed, and I loved this new place we finally arrived at. I snuggled back into his side and drifted off, because in his arms I was home.

CHAPTER 21

ALIVE AND KICKING

PRIMA

FINALLY, the night of my concert arrived. Billed as the "Alive and Kicking Concert," the air felt supercharged backstage.

Robbie, Sara, Charles, Mick, a few of my band members, backup singers, hair and makeup artists, and my seamstress all crowded into my dressing room wishing me luck, but it was too much. I needed space and time to myself, as was typical of my pre-concert routine.

I clung to Robbie and squeezed his arm, knowing the time was near for me to put on my costume and head to the stage.

"Do you get nervous before a concert?" He asked.

"Always, but it goes away through the middle of the first song as soon as I see my fans enjoying it."

"You'll do great, darling." He kissed my lips with a promise that it would all turn out fine.

And he was right, it would. Everything I'd been through with mom, with my ex, with a stalker fan, none of them could keep me down. I'd pushed through my fears and came out stronger in the end.

I stood on a nearby chair, with Robbie's hand steadying me. "Everyone. Thank you for being here. Your support has been amazing, and I love you all, but now, if you don't mind, I need a few minutes to myself to finish getting ready. I'll see you all out there. Oh, wait. Where's Mutt? Anyone seen Mutt?"

People looked around the room, but he wasn't among us.

"I haven't seen him today. He didn't return my texts earlier," Mick stated. "You'd think he'd be here for this."

"Want me to look for him?" Robbie asked.

"Please? I need to thank him. Especially after we argued yesterday. He's been a part of this process from the beginning. Even though he pissed me off more than once." I laughed and everyone did too, as they all shuffled out of the room.

My seamstress, Tabitha, stayed to help me put my first costume on, and at long last, I could wear the red dress that inspired my journey. My divorce celebration dress. I admired myself in the mirror; it was everything I'd hoped it would be.

"Stunning, sweetie," she cried, dabbing at her eyes.

"With a little room to spare. I could have eaten more cinnamon rolls, after all."

She grimaced. "Oh, how I worried everything would fit right. It's perfect."

We put on the white wedding gown over it, which was only attached with velcro so that in one yank at a certain point in my song, I could rip it off. My vision was complete. I sent a tiny prayer of thanks out into the universe for my muse.

"Anything else?" Tabitha asked after we took selfies together for our social media profiles.

"No. I'll stand here and breathe and try to take it all in. If you see Robbie, tell him I'm ready to be escorted to the stage. And thank you. Really. This and all the costume work you created so fast for me in time for this concert was above and beyond." We hugged tight.

"I'm so happy to have worked with you, Prima. Break a leg." She opened my dressing room door just as Andrew was about to knock. They scooted around each other, and he stood there with an enormous vase of colorful flowers in his hands.

"Ma'am, someone delivered these flowers for you."

"Oh thanks, and by the way, I know I was rather harsh to you and your Knights, but I really cannot thank you for watching over me the past month. You truly were my knights in armor and helped give me peace of mind through all of this."

"No problem. That's what we're here for." He set the flowers down on my dressing table.

"Tell your men I'll be happy to autograph something for them and they'll each also receive a copy of my album as a gift from me."

"Sure thing, and thanks." He grinned and resumed his post outside of my door.

A few years ago, a different me wouldn't have given one thought about the people that helped me, and that was probably why my entourage deserted me in Vegas last summer. Use enough people on the way to the top and they didn't stick around long.

Well, today marked a new era. The Prima era, the baddest bitch in rock—with a heart of gold.

I turned my attention to the flowers. "Must be from Robbie," I said under my breath, my heart skipping a beat for him.

I reached for the note, but a ping from my phone announced a message from Trevor. He was another person who deserved all my thanks.

> Trevor: Hey, wish I were there to see your concert tonight.

> Prima: Tour dates announced soon, and there'll be a few in California. You can be my guest at one. The least I can do to thank you for saving me that night after I ran from my mother.

Trevor: Awesome! Good luck!

Prima: Stay in touch.

All these powerful emotions overtook me as I stood here being back on top of the world with a new man I loved, a new album, a concert I was about to slay, and a new me.

I pulled the card from the beautiful bouquet of tropical flowers, bright colors of yellows, purples, and oranges in a variety of flowers. Then it hit me. These must be from Mutt.

How appropriate given his penchant for Hawaiian shirts. I chuckled until I opened the envelope, finding it contained not a card but a letter on white linen paper. Typed, the block letters at the top in black read: *I'VE LOVED YOU ALL THESE YEARS.*

An icy chill went down my spine and my eyes glued to the page as it fell from my hands to the floor.

A knock came at the door, and Robbie entered. "Darling, I can't find—What's wrong?"

I pointed to the paper and all the color drained from his face. He rushed to me, picked it up and inspected it, holding it by the corners.

"Read it," I whispered.

He took in a deep breath through his nose because of his clenched jaw and cracked his neck before he read it aloud.

Dear Prima,

Hey babe. You're getting ready for the concert that will mark the next chapter in your career, and I wish I were there, but I can't be.

You see, I'm a sick man, and I checked myself into a psychiatric facility in Nashville for help.

I fell for you the minute I met you all those years ago. When I look at you, I still see the young girl your mother brought to me to produce your first album. You were scared, vulnerable, but so fierce with a determination that told me you'd rise to the top.

I followed your career and put myself in the path to be available to produce your albums. You became my obsession. I tried to push aside my feelings for you, even tried marrying other women to replace you, but it was no use.

You were mine.

After my last wife left me, I let my obsession take over. But you wouldn't see me as anything more than a friend, collaborator, producer.

I didn't intend to scare you, but I came to the realization yesterday that I could never be what you desired. I was ready to hurt you, hurt Robbie. All kinds of sick thoughts went through my head. But I couldn't go through with it. I love you too much.

I'm getting help, and I hope I can finally put aside these feelings I've had for you for far too long.

Mutt

I swallowed hard, and hot tears threatened. "How could this be? Mutt has been my tormentor, my stalker all this time? The man I'd worked many hours with to produce my albums?"

"Darling, when it comes to people like this, nothing makes sense. But it's not your fault."

I cried, but carefully dabbed at the tears so I wouldn't remove my makeup, while Robbie called in Andrew and spouted off several orders that I wasn't even listening to. Something about calling for a search from here to Nashville, dusting the letter for prints, and on and on.

When we were alone in the room again, Robbie held me as tight as he could without ruffling my hair or dress.

"I should cancel the concert."

His head jerked back. "No, you shouldn't. Don't let him have the satisfaction of ruining this moment for you."

"But you don't understand. His name and work are allover this album as the producer. It'll forever have a negative connotation to the public eye once everything becomes public knowledge."

His head shook back and forth. "It's *your* music though, right? Your words, your tunes, representing your journey."

"Yes, of course."

"Then go out there and sing it, baby. If you don't, then Mutt's won. You're Prima, the diva, the feisty woman who belongs on that stage tonight. You've more than earned your place there these past few months. Show the world what you're made of."

I stared in the mirror for a minute longer, recalling myself as the young girl Mutt first met. I'd often looked up to him as a father figure, but he let me down tonight.

"What will happen to Mutt?"

"My guys are on it. We'll find him, and confirm his story, see if he's getting psychiatric help. Then it's up to you if you want to press charges or at least get a restraining order. Whatever you decide, I'm on your side."

My shoulders dropped, as if weighed down with sadness over the whole ordeal. Robbie came up from behind and filled in the mirror with me. He was my life now, my future. "Hey, I'm sure this was all a shock, but at least now we know who was behind all of this. You can live your life out from under the fear now. It's in my hands and I'll make sure he never again gets anywhere near you."

"I can't believe I met you through all of this. You've become the most important person to me, Robbie Boyd. My love. My protector." I smiled bravely through my heartbreak.

"That's my girl. Now, let's get you back on the stage where you belong and can rock the world." He held out his elbow for me.

"You're absolutely right. I do belong on that stage tonight—alive and kicking." I hooked my arm in his elbow.

"About time you think I'm right about something." He winked, and he led me out of the room and to the stage.

Waiting in the wings, we kissed once more. "By the way, I hope you know *you're mine*, not his," he said, referring to Mutt's letter.

The crowd chanted "Prima. Prima." Clapping their hands and stomping their feet, shaking the entire building.

"Well, I *am* yours...but I'm also *theirs*." I pointed to the fans. "Can you handle that, chief?"

He threw his head back and laughed. "Yeah. I can. I have no choice. Besides, they can have Prima, but I get Mellie all to myself. Now go on and break a leg."

The band walked on, assumed their positions, and the minute I appeared, the crowd roared the historic theater off its foundation. It took several minutes before they calmed down enough so we could start the first number.

In the bridal gown, I started out singing an old ballad that was all mushy gushy. Then the crowd leapt to their feet when I ripped off the gown, revealing the red dress of my dreams underneath. My first tune, a fast number with plenty of wild guitar riffs, delivered exactly the punch I'd planned.

As the concert went on, I could see it in the fans' faces how much my lyrics resonated about lost love, aching hearts, and dying dreams. When I burned a wedding album of photos on stage, they cried with me. When I toasted to my divorce papers with an actual glass of champagne, I then shook and sprayed the bottle of bubbly everywhere as they screamed and laughed with me.

We were one, my fans and I, mourning my loss and all of my challenges. And later in the show, when I hit them with my favorite love ballad, the one Mutt and I fought over...tears were everywhere on every face, including mine.

"That last one was for you out there. Yes, you, and you, and you. I see you. After loss, we mourn, but then there's always hope. I found hope again..." I glanced over at Robbie, my love, my protector waiting in the wings, and I skipped over to him and grabbed his arm. "Come on."

"Who me? Onstage?" He shook his head, but I pulled hard and he reluctantly followed.

I held up our hands together between us. "This is my hope!" I screamed into the mic and fans went wild. To him, I yelled in his ear, "Ready to give them something good to talk about? Kiss me."

"You sure?" Robbie asked.

Screw the paparazzi, hunting us down, wanting a photo of us kissing again or any photo of us together. Screw anyone trying to keep me under their control. I'd live life on my terms from now on, not theirs. "Oh yes. I love you."

To his credit, he did it up good, grabbing me, dipping me until my hair hit the floor. "I love you, too." His searing kiss went deep, our tongues twirling, my heart and soul yearning for him. The noise from the crowd was deafening; the entire event was a success, in my opinion, the only one that mattered.

Robbie let me up and from the smoldering heat in his eyes, I had no doubt that later he'd satisfy me tonight in bed. But I took one more look around the theater, and my soul felt completely satisfied for the first time in a long time. The success of this day, of my comeback, would live on in me forever.

"Thank you and goodnight!" I yelled, skipping off stage hand in hand with my man, my protector, my love.

CHAPTER 22

A LITTLE BOURBON, A LOT OF BLISS

ROBBIE'S EPILOGUE

PER MAC'S LAST WISHES, Kipp, Blake, and I took a trip deep into the hills and finally found his body in one of his favorite hunting spots. We wrapped him up and carried him out, the entire time sharing stories we recollected about him, often laughing, sometimes choking up. We all admired him as we grew up.

Because he'd prepaid his funeral expenses, we had him buried at the Kissing Springs Cemetery. He'd paid for three plots, one for him, one for his wife, and one for the daughter who'd gone missing years ago. We didn't know if we would ever fill those two plots, but we gave Mac a proper burial for his years of service as an officer and chief in the community.

After his funeral, I met with a lawyer to review his last will, and in it, he'd left the cabin to me. I felt touched and honored that I would get to keep a little bit of him with me. His wife had flown in for the reading of his will, but none of the daughters came, and not my ex. They got the rest of his belongings and insurance.

Prima and I agreed the cabin made a pleasant retreat for both of us. With her touring schedule and already at work on the next album, her career was taking off. But she kept her word that Kissing Springs would be her home base and flew back to me every chance she could.

I missed her on the days she was gone, but I finally got a passport and started taking some time off to travel with her to some of her European tour stops. The woman still drove me crazy in bed, and I'd do anything for her. But would she want more with me?

At the cabin, even as rustic as it was, when the weather cooperated, she could relax more on her visits. We enjoyed building a fire and sitting out with blankets together under the stars. We'd hike and enjoy nature, away from paparazzi and cameras and technology.

So we set to work planning on remodeling and improvements, and with the help of my buddies, Kipp and Blake, and even Charles and Dillon, we made slow but satisfying progress, taking pride in doing everything ourselves. Prima grew to love it as much as I did.

It took me some time before I could read the letter Mac had left me. The pain of losing him hurt too much at first.

Finally, one year to the day he drove away from his cabin, Prima and I spent the weekend there.

We sat on the porch and she watched over me while I drank an old bottle of his bourbon and read the letter.

Robbie:

I know the answers you seek about Fannie's disappearance. As I tell you this story, I know you will feel disappointed in me. You put me on a pedestal, thinking I was a good cop. I often heard you say that I'd inspired you to become an officer, that I'd mentored you.

Nothing makes me prouder than to see you and how far you've come.

But I have much to tell you now, through this letter, and you must understand I did what I had to do to keep the peace in Kissing Springs.

There was a time long before you were born, when I'd had more trouble with Ogden Montgomery's gang than I could handle. My officers were weak, and most of the good ones he bought off. The crime rate was way too high for a small town our size. Frankly, I became exhausted of it all. I considered quitting.

To make matters worse, Anthony Carloni, a Chicago mobster, decided he'd shift his drug, moonshine, and laundering operations throughout Kentucky, particularly keen on Kissing Springs. Well, old Ogden and his brother didn't take kindly to the mob boss's intrusion on their territory. The Montgomerys held a monopoly on the town for so long, now they were being challenged.

As I mentioned earlier, my officers were overburdened. I grew tired of the Montgomerys, and I certainly didn't have the resources to fight the power of the Chicago mob.

Anthony started coming to town more often, pushing his way into the area. Soon, we realized Anthony had somehow met Fannie Boyd, and they'd fallen in love. Fannie was a good girl, and I didn't know what she saw in him. We figured Fannie didn't realize he was a mobster. Had she known, she'd probably never have gotten mixed up with him.

One day, I got a visit from Ogden, begging for my help. Seems Anthony wanted to bridge the gap between Chicago and Kissing Springs and threatened to kill Ogden's family if he didn't go along with his plans.

Ogden said he'd make it all go away. He wanted the mob out of here as much as I did. All he needed from me was to look the other way.

Sure enough, he didn't tell me how, but he made it all go away. He said he "sent a message" to Chicago, and they never came calling in Kissing Springs again. The town returned to normal even though we still had to deal with Og's gang. The only problem was, Fannie went missing about the same time.

Then one day, several months later, Anthony turned up dead on the shores of the big Chicago river. But nobody ever found Fannie's body. Until now, decades later, when you extracted her body from under the foundation after the Brown Jug fire.

Fannie's death has been on my conscience all these years. I had no proof, but I believed Ogden had her and the Chicago fella disappear—how, I don't know. I'd given Ogden my blessing to do what he had to do to wash Chicago away from the shores of

Kissing Springs, never thinking he'd do something like this and hurt one of our own townsfolk.

I blame myself. As you know, being a cop, some decisions we make aren't easy, and some we don't talk about. I did what I did to get the town back under control, and it worked. If I hadn't, I truly believe the mob would have shrouded the town you love under a cloud of darkness and dirty deeds we might never have escaped.

Instead, we just had Ogden's gang to tolerate.

I suppose, if you wanted to, you could hunt down Ogden and see if he'd confess or something, but I doubt he would give you any answers.

Son, some things are better left in the past. If you dredge up the details, you might open a door for the mob to come back here and serve their own kind of justice on the town in retaliation for Anthony's death. And trust me, you don't want that.

Stay true to the badge or make your choice. Either way, you've been so good to me. I'm proud of you, son, and I'll be smiling back at you from Heaven.

Mac

"Are you okay?" Prima asked.

I squeezed her hand then folded the letter away. We rocked quietly on the porch for a while and I was grateful she gave me some space to think. So much had happened in the town of Kissing Springs since it's beginning. For such a small town, it certainly held more than its fair share of morally gray and dark history.

My sister, Meadow, had campaigned for a new future for the town and won, and made great strides as mayor seeing her changes through. Even though it hurt thinking how Fannie met with such a gruesome ending, I believed Mac was right.

What would dredging up the past accomplish? We didn't want the mob here, for sure. And it seemed Charles handled moving Ogden out of town somehow. Might there finally be peace in Kissing Springs after all these years? But could I live with letting the past stay buried?

I'd been a cop far too long, always believing things were either black or white. But maybe this time, I could be okay with the gray in between. It was time to look forward, not back, to grow and build a bright future, and with Prima by my side, I'd start tonight.

I got out of the rocking chair and got down on bended knee in front of her while producing a ring from my pocket. She gasped and held her heart.

"Prima, you've rocked my world from the moment I first met you. Would you marry me so we can rock it night and day for the rest of our lives? It's just a simple proposal, but you know I'm not all that flashy. I just hope you hear my heart in it."

Tears rolled down her cheeks before I even finished asking. "It's perfect. Short and sweet. Yes, a million times yes," she cried, and nearly knocked me off the porch, throwing her arms around me.

This cabin meant the world to Mac. Long ago, he'd told me this was his little piece of blissful Heaven.

It'd been a long time coming for me, but I think I finally found *my* bliss with Prima in my arms.

The End...

More Kissing Springs stories are on the way:

Thanks for reading the third book out of three in my portion of the Welcome to Kissing Springs Multi-Author Collection.

These characters have been so fun to write, and become such a part of my heart, from Meadow and Dillon, to Sara and Charles, and Prima and Robbie. What to read next:

The Knights continue to operate in Kissing Springs and get their own series of short stories, starting with My Hot Summer Knight.

Those stripping Santas from the Kissing Springs Derby Nights All-Male Revue Crew (From my book Single Santa) are now moonlighting as security guards...and when they have hot women around, they get really protective!

Blake Wilson (Search and Rescue) gets his own story in a related series in Kissing Springs coming in 2024.

How to Read Zee's Kissing Springs

Chronology

Start here:

Prequel to Welcome to Kissing Springs,

(written with Peggy McKenzie) Tells the origin story of the feud between the Montgomerys and the Boyds as it started in the 1800s.

Prologue to Single Santa

Read about Meadow Boyd's famous flannel bonfire incident after she broke up with her ex.

Single Santa

In this second chance romance, Dillon Montgomery returns to town and reignites the flame he once had with Meadow Boyd.

Mister Montgomery

Charles Montgomery's plans go awry in Single Santa, but can he redeem himself by being a hero for one night?

Sunshine & Secrets

Charles Montgomery moves back to Kissing Springs with his twin girls, hoping to start over and help Dillon in his business. He never expects to find love again until Sara Simms becomes his new nanny.

Bourbon & Bliss

Robbie Boyd loves his small town role as police chief, but when Sara's sister, Prima, comes to town, his small world goes crazy. But then, what does he expect from the wild rockstar diva?

My Hot Summer Knight

Those stripping Santas from the Kissing Springs Derby Nights All-Male Revue Crew (From my book Single Santa) are now moonlighting as security guards...and when they have hot women around, they get really protective!

More to come in the Kissing Springs world.

Visit the author's website for more information:

ZeeIrwinAuthor.com/KissingSprings

Welcome to Kissing Springs
Multi-Author Steamy Romance Series

Welcome to Kissing Springs, Kentucky!

In this new collection of steamy romance, multiple authors bring you standalone stories from single dads to second chances, ex-military to sports romances all set in the small town of Kissing Springs, Kentucky.

Santa Season:

Welcome to Kissing Springs

Sunshine Season:

Welcome to Kissing Springs: Sunshine Season

Bourbon Season:

Welcome to Kissing Springs: Bourbon Season

THE FATED LOVES SERIES

Billionaires from Boston, each possessively loyal, are fighting to protect the women they love.

"Humorous, heartfelt, and HOT!!!"
~Reviewer

One thing is certain, with these Fated Loves couples, there are plenty of steamy nights ahead.

Start with Book 1, This Is Fate.

Or Binge read the series now.

STEELE VALLEY BILLIONAIRES SERIES

What You Give, Book 1

A luxury resort, a billionaire, a burning out CPA—and a threatening corporate takeover. Can true love pave the way for a successful merger?

What You Take, Book 2

A billionaire, a single mom, a sweet emotional support dog, and a lake of mysterious waters—Can true love strike twice in Steele Valley?

Preorder: **What You Love coming 2024** (Wyoming's story)

THE OFF-DUTY RESCUE RANCH

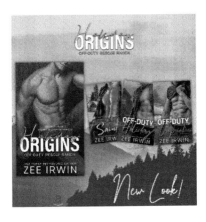

Three steamy, small town military romances provide the holiday origin story for the Off-Duty Rescue Ranch.

If you love hot former military men, strong women, and matchmaking horses, then start reading today.

Read each book in the series.

Read 3-books-in-1

RETURN TO GLENDALE FALLS SERIES

Love a steamy, small town romance series?

I never thought I'd find myself here again . . . back in this small town.

Returning home is never easy, and for these sisters they find out the secret:

Where the heart is, so is home.

Read *Return to Glendale Falls*, and join the Hale family of sisters as they navigate life, love, and triumph in the face of loss.

Ride It Slow

Dance In The Light

Kiss By The Moon - coming 2024

Also by Zee

The Fated Loves Series

Steele Valley Billionaires Series

Off-Duty Rescue Ranch: Holiday Origins Series

Return to Glendale Falls Series

Welcome to Kissing Springs: The Santa Series
Welcome to Kissing Springs: Sunshine Series
Welcome to Kissing Springs: Bourbon Series

Dark Hockey Romance

Stay in touch, and I'll have a free story for you:
ZeeIrwinAuthor.com/newsletter

About Zee Irwin

Hello from Zee!

Zee Irwin is a USA Today Bestselling Author who gets powered up by steamy small town romance. She's a bit of sunshine living countryside in Pennsylvania with her own grumpy alpha guy, two teenagers, and twin kitties. Her favorite character to write is a small town billionaire, especially if he falls first, is former military, and is possessive of the woman he loves.

Visit her at zeeirwinauthor.com/series to keep up to date on her latest work in progress.

- facebook.com/ZeeIrwinRomance
- instagram.com/authorzeeirwin
- amazon.com/author/zeeirwinromance
- pinterest.com/ZeeIrwin
- bookbub.com/authors/zee-irwin
- goodreads.com/zee_irwin

Made in the USA
Middletown, DE
29 September 2023

39131719R00128